SHADE TREE MAFIA

"THE LAST REAL SAGA"

By

Kenneth Thomas

Royals and Rebels Publishing

Shade Tree Mafia "The Last Real Saga"

Copyright © 2017 by Kenneth Thomas

DEDICATION

This book is dedicated to all family and friends who supported a journey that seemed impossible to many. Throughout the years, the love of the arts has tested life on every level. Though determination and faith in God all things are truly possible. To those who have truly sacrificed such as our parents, children and siblings that had to go without and worry what would come of this dream that was hard for anyone else to see, we thank you! We hope that through our dreams will come many blessings that may contribute to a brighter future for others. Such as the start of the B.O.L.F.F.A Foundation "Beacon of Light for Fallen Angels" a foundation that gives second chances to those who have been institutionalized as well as their family members. Through art comes blessing and we will never be able to thank you enough.

PREFACE

There's a Civil War on the horizon, and this time it's not the U.S. Government. The South's most powerful family in Organized Crime is about to lose its leader "Martin Delruso" to terminal cancer. Afraid to leave behind his daughter "Rebecca Delruso" and wife "Sharon Delruso" at the mercy of the New York Mafia, it's urgent that he find the son of his maid that passed away 25 years earlier. "Adrian Delruso" was adopted and raised by the Delruso family as one of their own but the powerful New York Mafia would rather go to war than answer to their new leader. The Delruso's know they cannot win a war against the North when the families combine as one, so "Adrian Delruso" makes an alliance no one will ever see coming. The son of a maid, poor adopted black kid from the south "Adrian Delruso" who is now the most powerful man in the Mafia and the son of a drug addict, poor white foster kid from the South who is now the most powerful man in the Aryan Brotherhood "HardRain" are on a collision course with the five Mafia families of New York.

TABLE OF CONTENTS

Dedication 3

Preface 4

1 I Rather Die Young 6

2 The Protector Within.................... 18

3 When a Hero Dies 33

4 Blueberry Skies 42

5 Cocoa Rain 52

6 Momma's Little Black Bastard 63

7 Shattered Glass and Red Roses 74

8 Rose Gold Chariot....................... 85

9 Me, Momma and God 99

10 A Dark Crossroad...................... 109

11 American Prom Queen 119

12 There's a Rage in Harlem 127

13 A Friend of a Friend.................... 136

14 She's Never Going Back 145

15 Southern Savage........................ 154

16 South Bound............................ 165

17 United Nations 173

18 Raining Down Guineas 182

19 Royals and Rebels 190

20 Welcome to My Zoo 204

21 40 Days of Demons..................... 221

22 Death from the Bayou 229

ONE

I RATHER DIE YOUNG

Like most blacks in my neighborhood, we were poor but my mother and father worked hard so it never seemed like it. We pretty much had everything we needed. Food, shelter, clean clothes and momma gave me plenty of love. Our neighborhood wasn't really the safest but everyone knew one another. Those who weren't blood related had such long history together it seemed like we were.

Of course, the same old 80's story, crack takes over the urban communities, a lot of racism is still apparent to everyone but as long as you stayed in your lane there really wasn't much trouble. We had a few people from our side of town that were interested in interracial relationships, that brought a little drama every now and then but overall most of the parents were strongly against it so it wasn't like an everyday thing.

We lived in a small town; it was just my mother and me most of the time. I know what you're thinking the typical hood story young kid grows up without a father, but my father didn't leave he passed away when I was young. My father was the local trash man. He worked for the city. I have some pretty rough memories of him. Usually, by the time I woke up in the morning, he was gone to work and by the time I went to sleep, he wasn't home yet.

On the weekends, I saw him but he was mostly at the local juke joints. He and some of the other elders in the neighborhood would shoot pool and have drinks pretty much the entire weekend. I learned a lot by watching them.

I was pretty much a man way before my time. My father had an old El Camino; it's kind of like a half truck, half car. On the weekends when he was too tipsy to drive, he would wake me up and I'd drive him over to the juke joints. I could barely see over the steering wheel but I'd put phone books and pillows in the driver seat, whatever it took so I could at least get a glance at the road and see the white lines. Occasionally I'd cross over the yellow line but he was too drunk to notice so I'd quickly snatch the wheel to get back in my lane. I was pretty much a nervous wreck but we made it.

Now that I'm older and I think back, those were some of the best times of my life. I knew everybody. All the older men from the neighborhood knew my name and would give me money to buy candy and tell me how much I looked like my father. The women would pinch my cheeks, give me hugs and to be honest, I loved the attention. My favorite song was Michael Jackson, Smooth Criminal. My dad would pass me his hat; I sat it by the pool table and would do the moonwalk while the elders would scream telling me how great I was at it. I'd take my hat full of money while some of the other kids looked on in admiration.

I think that was the first sign of trouble and I didn't know. I just loved the attention, but not as much as I loved being with my father. He was frail and I could see that life was getting to him, seems as if his body was exhausted. I was young but intelligent for my age, probably because of being around so many older people during my childhood.

I'd walk to the corner store that was a mile away just to hang with the older folks. I could see them laughing as I walked toward them with no shoes on. It would be the middle of the summer. The concrete was so hot you could see the steam coming from it. It didn't bother me, though. Actually, I liked the sting on the bottom of my feet. My cut off shorts that my father made me with the little Indian slits on the bottom of them that hung like tassels I hated those shorts. Seem like I had a thousand pair because every season all my winter pants became summer shorts. The kool-aid stains on the candy cane striped tee shirt mixed with a few dirt stains from playing football in the neighbor's yard made it obvious it was me. My tight curly nappy hair that was filled with gray dust from the high winds sweeping across the dirt roads was badly in need of a haircut.

When they saw me they would smile and call my name as they took sips from their 40oz beers and puffed on their Winston cigarettes. This one older man named Joe Lee was always sitting in the store and would have someone bring me a sausage dog and a grape soda then he would give me two dollars and tell me later I could get some now and later candy. They were my favorite type of candy to buy.

It's Saturday, the weather is beautiful, the night is coming and the cars are piling up and they're running out of space along the street to park. Seem like the whole neighborhood was tipsy. There was a fish fry at the baseball field earlier. The local boys won so everybody's hype. You can hear the music playing through the neighborhood. Juke Joints on every corner are full. Street lights are coming on so it's time for most of us young kids to go home.

I had three friends that I was close too. Chase, his family was from New York. He hated living in the country. Devon, he was kind of a good boy, a little scary, but he was family. Also, a white boy that lived on the other side of the neighborhood, his name is Whiteboy Vegas. We called him that because his dad was a heavy gambler and every time the old men would see him coming, they would yell out, "Here come Vegas." They didn't really like Vegas' dad. Everyone knew he was a racist but his gambling problem wouldn't let him stay out of the Juke Joint and they loved to take his redneck money.

He wasn't the best player. I used to always wonder how he made it out of there alive after saying words like nigger; he's upset because he lost all his money. My dad would tell me he pays for every word. A man words never hurt. What hurts more is when he goes home and tells his wife he lost all his money to a black man.

As Devon, Whiteboy Vegas and I started to walk we heard loud arguing coming from behind us. When we looked back down the road we could see this lady name Ms. Annie May screaming telling us to hurry up and get home. Not long after that, we heard a loud bang. As we ran back we could see everybody running in the same direction. The screams got louder only now they're mixed with cries.

As we got closer I could see from a distance it was Mr. Joe Lee's house. He was holding a shotgun. His 31year-old son was lying at his feet. There was blood all over the ground, it glazed the green lawn. You could see the moonlight bouncing off the bloody blades of grass. Mr. Joe Lee was screaming. "I told him to stay out of me and his mammy's business, that's my wife!" he shouted. That's when I realized that Mr. Joe Lee had shot and killed his own son. I guess him and Mrs. Betty Mae was arguing again.

Such a tragedy, but little did I know some of these lessons would follow me throughout my life.

These days kids get away with everything, talking disrespectful to their parents, even physically abusing them. Not back then! I remember my mom saying, "I'll kill you dead before you be around here thinking you going to jump on me." We all knew Mr. Joe Lee's son was only trying to protect his mom but we also all knew to let the police handle it. It was a sad situation because really, she may have been dead before the police got there.

We live about an hour from all the police stations. We never really called them anyway. We were kind of like our own police. As a matter a fact we were our own doctors, our own police, our own judge, our own jury, and now that Ronald Regan bringing all this crack up in here, we're our own bank! Everyone was hurt when Mr. Joe Lee killed his son and he also had to go to prison for it. It was kind of like we lost two family members at the same time. The cries seemed endless but we all know where there's a juke joint there's bound to be another altercation.

The summer is scorching hot; beautiful southern women are sundresses and big curls. With all the new-found wealth thanks to Ronald Regan, they turned country boys on tractors to cultured boys in Cadillac and Cutlass Supremes. They wore slacks, silk shirts, flat tops, and S-Curls. You could smell curl activator in every house you went in. Everybody's favorite day of the week was Sunday, a reason to dress up in your finest outfits and enjoy the show. The cars cleaned to a perfect shine and women walking the pavement off the street, with music coming from all directions. Everybody was happy and every family had a local drug dealer in it so everybody was eating ok.

The whites were happy, the blacks were happy the drug business was beneficial to everyone. The blacks knew how to get the cocaine to the area and whites had lots of lands to grow the marijuana.

Our small town was finally at peace. Our area has it all and now we have a reason to get along because any outsider is a threat to all our financial stability. I don't know if that makes us friends but it sure makes us allies. I always loved to see the people in my neighborhood happy. Of course, I could have no part in this adventure, I'm 9 years old and mama would kill me.

We didn't have a lot sometimes. I was afraid that our old house would catch on fire but overall I was happy. I was young I didn't know what life outside my neighborhood was like. The only place I ever been was school and maybe to the doctor once. Can't miss what you don't know exist. I was a natural Boy Scout. We made tents in the woods from branches and scraps of metal and board from the trash pile. We made bow and arrows from a branch and shoestrings or whatever rope we could find. We burned fires for the bugs and ate from the blackberry bushes by the briar patch. I guess you can say I was trained to live off the land if need be. I knew how to kill a deer and clean it. I was Ford tough for a kid, they made us wrestle and learn to fight. None of the elders wanted their kid to be considered a pussy. We played tackle football with the adults and believe me they didn't show us any mercy. This life wasn't much to a lot of people but to us it was paradise. The smell of fresh cut grass and honeysuckles was everywhere. We had ponds and rivers to fish and plenty of woods to play in.

If I had known then what I know now, dying young would not have been so bad. Over the years, the ponds turned to burial grounds and the rivers turned into an avenue to transport drugs. What once smelled like honeysuckles now smells of wino's and crack heads. You could have never convinced me that life would have taken the direction it has.

My father's health is steadily declining and I can see the concern in my mother's eyes. She's been a maid for 10 years now and I can tell she knows that if my father dies it won't be enough to take care of the both of us. I feel like my dreams are talking to me and at this point in my short life, I can see the future. Parts of me rather die young because what lies ahead doesn't seem so bright.

TWO

THE PROTECTOR WITHIN

I hated school! We had to wake up super early only to get there super late because we lived so far away. Summer is gone and so is the excitement. Everyone's inside hiding from the extremely low temperatures. I know when I get off the bus today it's the same routine, homework, then straight outside to chop wood with my father. I don't know what I hated more, having to chop wood at barely 100 pounds or watching my father gasping as he swung the ax.

My father was asthmatic and he smoked cigarettes heavy, as well as drank alcohol. Today he decided to give me the scare of my life as I stood behind him stacking wood on a little red wagon. I watched him in his red and black flannel checkered shirt, as he swung to split the wood he missed and fell forward. He hit the ground and grabbed his chest as he gasped for air. I could hear the wheezing coming from him. Instantly I turned to run for the front door as I screamed for my mother. I heard my father attempt to yell for me to come back. As I run back to his side my chest was pounding in fear. I finally realized that today is the day, I better toughen up. I helped him to his feet and he sits on a log and says to me, "Don't worry your mother." Crazy as it sounds I sat there inspired. Out of breath and freezing cold, the only thing on his mind was the concern of my mother.

That night as he loaded the wood heater I sat in silence pretending I was watching TV because there were a million thoughts running through my mind. I could feel my mother's energy as she watched me. In her heart, she knew something was wrong. The worrying look on my father's face pretty much was a tell all. As you know, having a wood heater sometimes means the rest of the house might be freezing cold. I lay in my bed watching the fog come from my mouth as I exhaled bundled under blankets in a hopeless attempt to stay warm.

With so much already on my parent's mind, I didn't want my father having to stay up all night reloading the heater so I just laid still and prayed I'd fall asleep soon. It didn't take long because before you know it I was thinking I had died and gone to heaven because I could smell hot breakfast cooking. I heard my momma's voice say, "Baby it's time to get up." I didn't want to move afraid that when I walked in the kitchen it would have all been a dream and it would be some kind of tragedy waiting for me. As I slowly walked towards the bedroom door, I peeped around the corner and made eye contact with my father who said, "Get the molasses out your ass boy. Didn't you hear your momma call you?" The fear in my heart let me know it wasn't a dream so I began to smile. I rushed to the table and ate until I was full. Once momma gave me a cup of koolaid with breakfast, reality set in. Something is really wrong! I didn't say anything, I was just glad it was Saturday and I was going out to play with my friends.

As soon as I was finished I brushed my teeth, washed my face, grabbed my coat put on sneakers and burst out the door I set out looking for adventure. I played basketball the entire day with Devon and Whiteboy Vegas.

We were filthy but we were doing what we loved to do. Every once in a while, we would see Vegas' brother HardRain drive through the neighborhood looking for him. He hated when Vegas came around us. HardRain was a self-proclaimed racist. The total opposite of Vegas, but their entire family was with the Aryan Brotherhood. It scared my mom and dad that Vegas and I were such good friends. Everybody knew how dangerous his family could be but me being a kid it didn't bother me. Besides, everyone knew my mom and her side of the family was deep in the drug trade. So as much as the Aryans hated Vegas hanging out with the black kids they didn't want to upset the balance of things because they were making a ton of money.

So much that people not from our neighborhood were taking notice. You could feel the tension in the air. The adults had begun whispering a lot and acting nervous when strange cars would ride through. It was business as usual but all of us kids were getting these strange talks from our parents. Talks like, "Don't walk alone". This is our neighborhood we all family so with that being said we know something is wrong. Mama would now come get me before it got dark when I use to walk home by myself. There was always someone standing outside till all the kids got home so I didn't know why she was acting so protective.

When I got home I could tell she was upset so I didn't say much. I just went to take my bath and tried to get settled in before the Sunday night movie comes on. I got in my bed and reached in my pocket pulled out my pack of now and later candy. I must have dozed off because I was awakened by loud screaming.

I heard people yelling in the living room and things falling and breaking on the floor. My heart started racing as I heard my mother's voice I rushed toward it. I saw two men and my older cousin holding my father up while my mom was throwing things off the couch to make room for him. Stuck in a terrifying daze I saw blood shooting from my father's button-up shirt like a water hose. His shirt was drenched in blood as if someone tossed a bucket of water on him. As they laid him on the couch my mind was telling me to run back to my room but my heart made me rush to my father's side. The elders were pushing me back but my hand reached my father's shoulder, I felt the wetness from the blood that soaked his shirt. I fell backward onto the floor and looked at my fingertips stained in red. I quickly recovered and stood up looking on as they called the ambulance while my mother applied pressure to my father's wound.

I could hear the chatter coming from outside. The people from the neighborhood started to gather in the yard. When the ambulance took my father out I didn't follow them I returned to my room and sat in a corner by my dresser and began to cry. From all the commotion, I was sure I would never see my father again. I fell asleep in that exact corner drowsy and bloody, I felt someone lift my body and place me into my bed. I was very tired but I caught a glimpse of my mother's face with swollen eyes from crying and a runny nose from the cold room. She laid me down and covered me with a blanket. When she lay beside me I was too afraid to ask about my father so I curled up against her and pretended to be sleep. I could hear her hum lyrics from a Shirley Caesar song.

When I woke up that morning the neighbor was there, she took me to church. I didn't pay much attention that day.

I really wanted to know if my father was OK. I had asked the lady watching me where was my mother, the only thing she said was, "She'll be back soon." Pretty much that told me to mind my business so I didn't ask any more questions. I just sat angrily and pretended that I was listening to the preacher.

When the service was over I remember watching the lady, wishing she would hurry up and stop talking to everyone that passed by. It seemed that she would never stop talking. I figured if I didn't communicate with anyone and just sat on the steps as if I was irritated she would get the hint that I wasn't happy and then we would leave. Sure enough, she walked over and grabbed me by the hand. Everyone stared at me as we walked to the car. By the looks on their face, I began to lose more hope that my father would ever come home.

As we pulled up in my mother's driveway I could see her standing on the porch reading a piece of paper. As I struggle to open the car door and step out into the yard I

could hear her say, "There's my baby. I missed you so much."
I ran up to her and hugged her, she hugged me, took me by
the hand as she yelled to the lady who watched me, "Thank
you so much." When we walked into the house I exhaled and
started to tear up and sniffle as my father sat on the couch
bandaged up with a blanket around his shoulders. He
chuckled, "Thought the old man was gone didn't you squirt?"
As I hugged him he got tense because of the pain from his
wounds. When I glanced over at my mother her tears were
fighting against her smile to see which would take over the
look on her face. She wiped her tears away and said, "I'm so
glad we're all together again."

Over the next few weeks, my father healed and was
back in the yard chopping wood in no time. You could see
clearly life was taking its toll. His smiles that use to be pure
joy seemed to turn to exhausted smiles that were clearly
hiding the pain. It seemed like that winter month lasted
forever. It was nice to see the daisies popping up through the

brown grass. It wasn't summer time yet, but a few colors peeking through the gray days were something we kind of needed around here.

My father was working in the yard and told me to take the gas jug and walk up to the corner store and get gas for the lawnmower. I could smell the burning leaves which I really enjoyed. As I took off down the railroad tracks, gas jug in hand and a pocket full of pennies it's an exciting day for me. I get to play with the lawn mower and I have enough pennies to get me two packs of now and later candy. In a distance, I saw two men talking, they were fishing in the water hole beside the railroad tracks. "Hello," I said. Then I went on my way, when I got to the store I paid for my gas and now and later candy. I could overhear some of the elders in the back whispering. "Son, be careful walking on them tracks by yourself, why don't you take the other way around on your way back home," said the one with the gold tooth in the front. "Yes sir," I replied. "Why he got to take the long way for, the tracks are much shorter?" The other man with the hunter's camouflage hat on asked. "The fool that stabbed that damn boy daddy down there in that fishing hole, now you take another way, you hear me boy?" The man with gold tooth said sternly. As I turned and walked toward the door, I didn't look back, all I could feel was anger and fear what if my father came looking for me and he took the railroad tracks to get here.

I dropped the gas jug and jogged home at a fast pace. I heard the car horns blow as people said hello when they passed by. I didn't speak; my mind was focused on one thing. When I reached my mom's yard, I could see my father in the back by the trash pile so I went through the front door. I called my mother's name to see if she was inside and she didn't respond so I peeked out the window and saw her in the front yard watering her plants. Instantly something came over me, a paralyzing fear of this man being so close to my father who clearly hasn't healed yet. Suddenly I had an idea.

I ran to my father's room, went into the closet and found his tackle box. I took the tackle box with me and ran back toward the tracks. I could see the two men fishing from a distance; the steam from the sun was bouncing off the iron bars on the railroad track. "How are you doing little fella?" said the man as I got closer. I stopped and stared at him. "Are you from around here?" he asked. I stood silent and continued to stare. My knees became weak, my hands started to tremble; I started to sweat and became extremely nervous. He reached in his pocket so I took a step backward and put the tackle box on the ground in front of me. He pulled his hand out and I could see two wrinkled dollars. He handed them to me. "Here you go youngin," He said in a sarcastic way. The gentleman with him was quiet and stared in amazement as if he knew, that I knew who they were. As the man took another step towards me, I quickly reached inside the tackle box. I pulled out a .25 caliber pistol that belonged to my father. The man stopped dead in his tracks as he looked at me nervously and fearful, it gave me power. Every moment of that night my father was stabbed seem to come rushing back into my head. "Easy little man," the man said as he stood nervously in front of me. I clenched my teeth in anger. "Let's talk about this," he said with a raised voice. I tilted my head to the right and pulled the trigger (Bong!)

The gun was so loud my right ear went silent. All I could feel was a warm feeling in my hand and a painful throbbing. It felt as if the gun had ripped my hand from my wrist. When I looked down, I could have sworn my hand would be on the rocks. His friend shouted loud, "Oh my God, what are you doing boy?" I wanted to pick up the gun again but I got nervous, opened the tackle box and kicked it back in with my foot. I locked it and took off down the tracks.

As I approached the yard my mom and dad stared in fear. My dad begins to run towards me. They had heard the gun shot but they didn't know where it had come from or know who was hurt. "What's going on?" he screamed. "I killed him!" I shouted. He grabbed me by the shoulders and started shaking me. "What are you talking about?" he shouted. "The man dad, the man that stabbed you!" I screamed. When he looked on the ground the tackle box was tipped over. There was fishing hooks, fishing lines, a box cutter and his .25 caliber pistol. The look on his face was pure terror. "Get rid of it," he said to my mother as he started running toward the rail road tracks. My mother grabbed me by the hand and ran toward the front door. She made me sit on the couch while she ran into the back room. All I could think now was my father is down there with this man who's dead and his friend is still alive. At that very second, there was a gunshot; it seemed to echo through the entire neighborhood. As I looked out the screen door, I could hear momma say, "Oh my God," as she ran up behind me. I could see a few of the men from the neighborhood run towards the tracks. My mother took me and sat me down on the couch and explained to me how the family business is to never leave the house. "What happens in this house stays in this house," she said.

I didn't see my father for the rest of the afternoon. As I was getting ready for bed, I was walking down the hall to throw my dirty clothes in the hamper only to run into him. When I looked at him his clothes were filthy, his hands were muddy and he was sweaty and tired. The only thing he said was, "When you wake up tomorrow son, today never happened." We never spoke about it again.

THREE

WHEN A HERO DIES

When I woke up this morning things seemed a bit stranger than usual. The house was quiet and my parents were already gone. The next-door neighbor was there. It was still dark outside. I washed my face, brushed my teeth and got dressed as usual. As I started out the door to the bus stop my neighbor passed me my lunch bag. I didn't really think about it much. We had a field trip that day. I was a little bit excited. We are going to the aquarium today. I've never been there but the other kids told me about all the animals they had, plus on field trip days my mom goes out of her way to make sure I have the best lunch.

When I got to school everyone was on the playground. I skipped breakfast that morning, I was too happy to eat. Some of the other kids and I that was in my class stood on the playground and talked about all the different animals we couldn't wait to see. When the bell rang we all rushed to class. The teacher did a roll call and collected our homework from the previous day. While I was looking through my backpack to gather my things, the principal knocked on the classroom door. When the teacher walked over she spoke to him and then glanced back at me, they called me over. All the other kids yelled,

"Ooooooooooh, you're in trouble." I got nervous but I knew I hadn't done anything wrong so I skipped over. The principal told me to grab my backpack that I had to go with the guidance counselor. At that moment, I got a little scared.

We went to the office and my neighbor Ms. Alice was there. I was surprised to see her. "Hi," I said with a confused look on my face. "We have to go but I'll bring you back later your mom needs you to come home," she said as she stood and hugged me. On the way home, I stared out the window hoping we would hurry back before everyone

leaves. I don't want to miss our trip. As we pulled into the driveway there were cars parked along the street and in the yard.

As I got out of the car I walked quickly towards the door focused on getting back as soon as possible. My mother met me as I reached for the handle. When I looked up her eyes was swollen and full of tears. It was hard for her to talk. She was trying to catch her breath, "Come in the back room with me, I have to talk to you," she said. As we walked the room started to move in slow motion. The neighbors started saying hello as I walked past. My eyes were noticing there was a bloody white handkerchief on the coffee table, several bottles of prescription medications on top of the TV, a ripped off hospital band on the kitchen floor and the bedroom was in disarray. There were papers and plastic tubing and in the corner was an oxygen tank. There was a hospital bed against the wall and a whole lot of boxes.

My mom sat me on the bed and she stared at me. "Where were you this morning when I woke up, Ms. Alice had to take me to school?" I asked. "Last night I had to take your father to the hospital, he wasn't feeling well," she replied. "What's wrong with him?" I asked. "He has Prostate cancer." "What does that mean?" "It means he's been sick for a long time and he wasn't getting better," she replied. "Where is Dad now?" I asked. "We tried to bring him back home and he started throwing up really bad and coughing up blood so I had to call the ambulance." My eyes begin to water up. I could feel her squeezing my hand. As the tears begin to roll down my cheek she broke down and begin to cry really hard and said, "Your father died on the way back to the hospital."

Suddenly I became paralyzed in pain, utter disbelief. My father was a hero, even if to no one else, he was to me. I stared at my mother shattered into a million pieces and I can't even begin to figure out how to put her back together again. I took her hands and put them on my face and said the only thing my little brain could think of, "You got me, mama." She put her forehead against mine, "I sure do sweetheart," I wiped the tears from her face grabbed my mother by the hand and walked her back into the living room with our guest.

While she talked to everyone I began to pick up things around the house I knew how neat mom liked things. I figured it would make her feel better, besides I know looking at the bloody handkerchiefs was making her feel worse. It seemed like I heard I'm sorry for your loss so many times it continued to ring in my head when everyone left. My mom is laying down now and I feel like I've been cleaning for hours.

The phone rang so I eavesdropped beside mama's door hoping it wasn't any more bad news. I don't know if things could possibly get any worse but no matter what the bad news was, it definitely wouldn't help. "Well they all pretended they loved us but now that he's gone we going to see how much they love us now, I'll be surprised if anyone one even come by to check on us anymore," said mom. She sounded so sad and I could hear the worry in her voice. As the weeks turned to months I came to realize she was right. They would speak to us and occasionally stop by to ask a question and sometimes glance through the house. When they leave, mom would look angry and say, "Nosey strumpets want something to talk about."

I remember one Sunday morning as we were getting ready for church mama was in such a great mood. I'm happy because she's happy. The gospel music is playing loud, and she has her favorite wig on. She gives me five dollars to put in the collection plate at church. She walks back to the bedroom to get her hat. While I'm waiting for her I hear the big trucks pull up, they've been working on the roads all week and I love to see the dump truck going back and forth.

Today it just didn't happen to be a dump truck. It was a tow truck and there was some scruffy looking man with dirty blue jeans, brown boots and a striped color shirt putting a chain up under dad's car. I screamed, "Mom!" As loud as I could and she came running almost falling down, her nerves haven't been the same since my father died. "What's wrong baby?" she shouted. "There's a white man trying to steal dad's car!" I yelled. "Wait here a second don't come out you hear me?" shouted Mom. She grabbed her purse and rushed outside yelling "hold on, hold on!" The white man shrugged his shoulders and continued to hook Dad's car to the chain. I saw my mama pull out a hand full of balled up bills and gave it to the man, but he continued and shook his head no.

I slowly lifted the window up so I could hear what was happening. "I'm sorry Miss but you're two payments behind, there's nothing I can do," he said. My mama started to cry. My anger got the best of me and I disobeyed her rushing onto the front porch. By the time I got there mama was on her knees crying and begging. "Please sir, please I'm begging you don't take our car how we going to survive without it?" she cried out. "Mama!" I screamed. "Stay right there baby," she shouted. "Sir that's my only way to work, don't you see how far we live out here we going to surely starve you take that car," she said with tears running down her face. The man once again shrugged his shoulders "Sorry miss I'm just doing my job."

As he pulled off slowly mom began to dust the dirt from her palms, her tears mixing with sweat pouring down her face. As my eyes followed the tow truck pulling our car slowly down the road I saw several of the neighbor's window blinds closing. I walked over to my mother and picked her up off the ground and helped her dust her dress off. I took her inside, sat her on the couch and went to get her blanket. When I covered her up she said, "Things are going to get a little tight around here for a while honey but

God going to see us through."

FOUR

BLUEBERRY SKIES

Well, I'm only 10 years old but I'm the man of the house now so that means I got to earn. Mama said she's taking me to work with her today so I guess this would be the best time to ask Mr. Delruso can I work on his blueberry farm. My mom worked for a family that was very wealthy and very much respected in our town.

Mr. Martin Delruso was a heavy set older Italian man with a bushy gray beard. His wife Mrs. Sharon Delruso was a beautiful older lady with blonde and silver hair. Their daughter Rebecca Delruso was my age, well a year younger than me she was nine. Mom had worked there since I was born but she knew the Delruso family for a very long time.

Mom and Mrs. Sharon both grew up here; mom would work weekends for her mother so she and mom became the best of friends. Today will be the first time I meet my mom's boss I'm kind of nervous because when I see him around town he always looks mean. There's no time for fear though if I don't work in this field this summer we going to starve this winter. I got to wait until the perfect moment to approach him because if mama catches me she's going to tear my hide to pieces.

My mother always had a lot of pride so even though it was extremely hot out today before she would ask the neighbors for a ride she packed us some water and some food, grabbed some sweat rags and we were out the door. Mama was walking like she was about to win a prize. The first ten minutes I was excited and ready to go, the next ten minutes I started reconsidering and right after that I was wonder was mama turning a little crazy. Sweat was pouring off her like water, the curls in her wig were gone and I couldn't get my tongue unstuck from the roof of my mouth. I didn't even know if I was walking anymore or was she dragging me. All I know is she had me by the wrist, and my Velcro sneakers were scrapping across the rocks the next thing I know we were on the Delruso's front porch.

I heard a white man yell out "Come on in here Azzy it's hotter than a whore's bible out there." Everybody calls mom Azzy but her name is Azure, it's pronounced like "as you're" walking. That's why dad married her he said he couldn't forget her name. Seeing Mr. Delruso for the first time was very intimidating. He's loud, aggressive and a pretty big guy. "Adrian! So you're the one Azzy brags about all the time?" Mr. Delruso asked. I stepped close to my mom, I was nervous because not only is he scary, I never been in a white person house before. Mrs. Sharon came around the corner right on time, any longer I'm sure between the heat and this huge white man yelling I was about to pass out. "Hi Adrian, I'm Sharon your mom told me a lot about you, are you thirsty would you like something to eat?" she asked. I looked at my mom hoping she give me the go ahead because I was dehydrated and one step away from turning to dust. "Go ahead on baby," said mom. As I sat at the table Mrs. Sharon poured me a big glass of apple juice and I drank it like there wasn't another drop left on earth. When she looked up, she noticed my mom staring at me with tears in her eyes. "Martin, can you come here for a second I need you to make Adrian something to eat while I talk with Azzy in private?" she asked yelling through the kitchen. "Adrian, you know I got a daughter about your age, she's out playing in the fields after you eat you can go play a bit." "Yes ma'am thank you for the apple juice," I replied. "You're welcome honey." Then enters the big scary white man, "Is everything ok Sharon?" he asked. "Yes honey," Mrs. Sharon replied. He glanced over at my mom "Azzy what's wrong?" The look on his face didn't really help my case of bad nerves. "Everything's fine honey," Mrs. Sharon answered as she grabbed my mom by the hand and dashed out of the kitchen.

"Adrian, you like PB and J?" asked Mr. Delruso. "Yes," I replied. "Everybody likes PB and J," he said. A few seconds later I heard the screen door shut really loud, sounded like it was coming from the back of the house. A young girl walks in about my height. "Hi dad, where's mom?" she asked. "She's in the back room with Azzy." "Yay Nana's here!" she shouted. "Rebecca this is Adrian, Azzy's son, and Adrian this is my daughter Rebecca," Mr. Delruso replied. I have to admit even though I was nervous it was nice to see some smiling faces.

Rebecca and I headed out back I was a bit cautious. I didn't want to get mom in trouble or myself either. I have never seen a house like this, it was really nice. The floors were sparkling, I could see my face in them. I wondered if they ever sat on the furniture because it all looked brand new. The kitchen had two stoves and they didn't even have to use matches to light it. Rebecca's room looked like the one from the movie kid with Tom Hanks. All the white people in the pictures looked so happy. I wondered if they knew any of the white people that were so happy on the television show star search. The house smelled like fresh laundry mixed with brownies. All of a sudden, I was really anxious to go outside and play because if I broke something mama is sure going to lose her job.

As we walked towards the back door I could hear all types of loud noise. I guess Rebecca could tell by the look on my face I was a little afraid. "Come on Adrian don't be scared it's just those stupid machines making all that stupid noise I hate it!" she shouted as she grabbed me by the arm. When the door opened, it was like Rebecca had her own Tonka store they had everything I couldn't help but scream, "Wow!" There was a dump truck, bulldozers, tractors, big wheel trucks it was like a dream. I looked at Rebecca with the biggest grin on my face and started shaking my head. "What," she asked? All I could think was if she doesn't like these big trucks then girls must be stupid in all colors. "Come on" she yelled! She ran out into the yard with me trailing behind.

As I looked I could see it, there were fields and fields and more fields of nothing but the most beautiful blueberry trees. The sun reflected off the berries like broken glass, my mouth began to water as I grabbed handfuls and shoved them into my mouth. They popped like a mouth full of plastic bubbles and sweet juice instantly filled my jaws. As they burst the juice ran down my chin. There was so much blue it seemed as if the sky was raining down around us. The scent filled my nose, the taste filled my mouth and the color filled my eyes.

We ran down the rows screaming to the top of our lungs with our arms spread wide. It seemed like we were going so fast that the blueberry trees were becoming blueberry walls everything was blending together. Rebecca fell down and I was running behind her so I tripped over her. She started wheezing and laughing hysterically "that was fun I need my asthma pump," said Rebecca. I was asthmatic to I got it from my father and luckily I had an inhaler. I pulled it out and started to wipe the mouthpiece off with my shirt but she snatched it and took to puffs. When I looked up I saw several white men who worked in the field staring at us. Three of them looked angry and two of them shook their head in disgust. Rebecca got her second wind and grabbed my arm again and took off full speed ahead darting right through the angry men. I felt if a girl isn't afraid then I'm not either so I screamed louder and laughed louder.

After running in the fields all afternoon, the sun began to set, the night was slowly covering the fields like a blanket. I heard my Mom and Mrs. Sharon scream for Rebecca and me so we ran towards the house. My mom was smiling and so was I because it was nice to see her feeling better. "My goodness you two are filthy look like you have been rolling in the dirt," said mom. "We have

Nana!" Rebecca screamed. "I tripped down and then Adrian tripped over me then I couldn't breathe because I didn't have my inhaler so I used his," she explained in one breath. Honestly, I got a bit nervous than, "So Adrian's our hero for today, yay!" Mrs. Sharon shouted. I looked at mom, smiled and asked was she ready to go home she looked at me, "We are home honey," she said. Mr. and Mrs. Delruso decided instead of my Mom having to walk to work every day it would be best if we moved into the guest house in their back yard. My mom was one of those tough southern women with a lot of pride so she insisted Mrs. Delruso take rent out of her check each month. She was making more money now since she was pretty much on the clock twenty-four hours a day. Rebecca screamed in delight because she loved having Mom around all the time. I didn't really complain because it was the first time I felt safe since my father died. Rebecca yelled

out "cool I have a big brother now!" Everyone smiled and so

did I.

FIVE

COCOA RAIN

They say time flies when you're having fun and it certainly does. I was 10 when I arrived at the Delruso home and now I'm the big thirteen. Rebecca is twelve she turns thirteen in two weeks. She's lucky her birthday is in the first week of summer break. We're excited because we are teenagers now and we go to high school next year. Middle school was a breeze, I had fun and it wasn't so bad for a majority white school.

I missed my friends from the old neighborhood; I didn't get to see them as much. I saw Whiteboy Vegas in the grocery store a few weeks back it was nice too. Other than his uncle Jared looking at me like he could hang me from the highest tree. You should have seen the way they looked at Mrs. Sharon. The rumor around town was Mrs. Sharon treated her help too good, but we didn't worry about it much. After all, it didn't seem like a job anymore it seemed more like a regular family.

We ate together, went to church together and did all the family activities together. Life was pretty good, even though people would purposely say things that were hurtful, and make sure it was loud enough so mom and I could hear it. It wasn't just one side either; it was both, the blacks and the whites. My mom was a very religious woman so she believed in turning the other cheek. Me, on the other hand, I was religious but I believed in looking them in the eye so they would know I knew how they felt. My dad always use to say, "People don't know how you feel unless you tell them." I was too young to say anything to the adults because mama would surely spank me but I'd sure give them a look. Not angry looks either, Dad said, "Showing a man your anger lets him steal your joy," so I'd give them more of a sinister look with my eyes and more of a kool-aid grins with my smile. Boy that always pissed them off. Sometimes when mom and I were in the store, the whites would whisper the word nigger as they passed by. If I was with Mrs. Sharon and Rebecca they would whisper nigger lover. They would never do it when I was with Mr. Delruso, they would just speak or stop and say hi as if they didn't call me names the last time they saw me.

The blacks weren't really any better. Mom would make me pick blueberries in the summer to help pay for my school clothes, and the blacks would say, "Master making sure you know your place, isn't he?" They would see my mom and say things like, "Azzy I didn't know you liked white meat," or "I didn't know Mr. Delruso like sleeping with the help." We all tried our best to ignore it but sometimes were harder than others.

It's the last week of school and there's a dance coming up. The weather is amazing and the entire eighth grade is excited. We never have to see this middle school again. Rebecca has three friends she knew since kindergarten, they were all very close. Amanda was a blonde prissy type, sort of diva and very arrogant. Leslie was a brown-haired girl; she was wild and loud all time. Alex, she was devious, always had the coolest parties and she loved to be the center of attention. Alex's father was the Mayor, they were very wealthy and they loved to show it and this party their having to kick off this summer shall go down in history. Mom, Mrs. Sharon and Rebecca spent all Saturday morning looking for the perfect dress and getting their hair done. It was a special girl's day out.

Mr. Delruso took me to the barbershop and to get new shoes. He asked did I have a girlfriend and made jokes the entire way home. There's a certain girl that caught my eye but I didn't really want to talk about it. I decided I would ask him how he and Mrs. Sharon first met. "I went up to her and just laid one right on the kisser," he laughed, "Seriously, when I laid eyes on that woman, I knew that either I'd have her or die without her, so I was patient and I showed her what a good guy I was and eventually, she couldn't live without me," he said proudly.

I thought about that the entire afternoon. As I was getting dressed I could hear that mom and Mrs. Sharon was excited, they were so happy. Rebecca was screaming through the house, you could feel her excitement through the walls. We were growing up. Our middle school years were about to be behind us. When we were ready we walked out onto the porch and Mr. Delruso took a ton of pictures. Rebecca was dressed in a white summer dress with yellow and orange stripes and had a white sheer scarf over her long flowing brown hair. She had on a new pair of white Mary Jane's on that she loved. It was windy that day. I loved how the wind blew up my red alligator shirt. Rebecca was laughing saying it looked like I had muscles. I reached in the pocket of my khaki pants and pulled out my pack of banana now and later candy and gave Rebecca one.

We walked to the car. You could tell both of us were clearly nervous. Mrs. Sharon got in the driver's seat and mom in the passenger. Mr. Delruso snapped pictures until the car was out of sight. As we pulled up to Alex's house you can see the cars lining up from a distance as all the kid's parents were dropping them off. You could hear the music from up the block. Rebecca was smiling from ear to ear. "I think I'm going to burst I'm so excited mom," screamed Rebecca. As we got out the car my Mom and Mrs. Sharon told us to be careful and to be waiting outside when they picked us up at 10:00pm. "Mom we're going to high school for God sakes, let us stay out until 11:00pm at least, that's what time the party's over," Rebecca complained." Mrs. Sharon looked at Mom and they agreed "Fine, have fun," Mrs. Sharon replied.

As we walked into the yard it seemed like the entire eighth grade was there. Everyone was in groups. The cool kids, the Goth kids, the brains and the future screw ups of America. When Rebecca saw Alex, Amanda and Leslie she gave me a hug and said, "Bye bro," and quickly ran off. Honestly, with all the groups I didn't know which one I really fitted into because I was surely the only one from my side of town.

When I walked through the house I saw two kids spiking the punch, and when I stepped in the back yard I could smell the stench of marijuana. All I could think about was for these to be rich white kids; they don't seem too different from the people in my old neighborhood. Everyone was happy, I'm not sure if it was the summer or the alcohol and weed, but it was a good time.

When the night came, the guys started navigating toward the girls. In the corner of the backyard I could see Alex talking to a group of the high school kids. She had a crush on a guy named Joey Middleton. He was a

sophomore with a bad attitude. He'd always come by on his dirt bike speeding down the road. He was on the basketball team and he was always in the newspaper. Every time she would look at him, you could tell she was hopelessly in love.

Amanda had broken away from the crowd and sat beside me on the picnic table at the side of the house in front of the driveway. Some of the other kids were playing basketball in the street which is where my attention was. Every time I tried to get up and go play Amanda decided she had another secret to tell me, or decided she wanted to confess her love for me. Things were starting to get a little chaotic; I think the alcohol was starting to kick in. All the kids knew that the next day they would be grounded by their parents but nobody cared. I did though, because my mom wasn't like most of the moms from this side of town.

They might get grounded but I might get put in the ground.

It was almost time for mom and Mrs. Sharon to return to pick us up, so I began to look for Rebecca. As I surveyed the front yard I didn't see her so I went inside the house and didn't find her there either. When I went into the backyard I saw Alex, she was with Leslie and a group of the high school guys. Joey was snickering and when I looked back at Amanda it seemed like it was hard for her to look me in my eyes. So I approached Alex "Have you seen Rebecca?" I asked. "No," she said. It was unlike Rebecca to disappear without checking in with me. The last three years of our life we told each other everything and I don't know what I'm supposed to tell mom and Mrs. Sharon if they get here and Rebecca's nowhere to be found.

I remember my father use to tell me, whenever we went to a large store that if we got lost go to a corner of the store because in the corner you could see everything so I went to the corner of the yard and as I scanned the yard full of people I noticed a lump in the flower bed on the side of the house. There were a few kids gathered around it and the crowd was slowly growing I squinted my eyes and walked closer. I saw a flicker of light and heard some of them laughing. The closer I got I could hear someone groaning and coughing. As the lump came into focus I saw that the flicker of light was the moon reflecting off the tip of Rebecca's white patent leather Mary Jane's. My heart begins to race. As I looked down, I saw that her dress was covered with dirt, her face was painted black, and she had a sign pinned to her dress that said, "Nigger Lover" and a noose around her neck.

I've never seen her drink before but something was clearly wrong. She couldn't move, as I picked her head up she mumbled my name. I tried my best to get her to her feet.

She kept falling so I had to scream at her so she would snap out of it. I put her arm around my neck and we staggered to the end of the yard to wait for Mrs. Sharon and Mom.

Rebecca was disoriented and I didn't feel safe at all. "Adrian, can you go in the kitchen and make me some cocoa I'm freezing?" she asked. I didn't want to alarm her so I tried not to let her hear me cry as I put her arm back around my neck and we slowly staggered down the street. I could see Mom and Mrs. Sharon coming towards us. The tears coming down my cheeks, poured so hard that the headlights from the car flickered off my face. Rebecca glanced over at me, "Adrian we're going to be sick it's really raining hard," she said. It never rained a drop that night Mom and Mrs. Sharon went into panic mode when they saw us. They quickly put us in the car and we sped off.

SIX

MOMMA'S LITTLE BLACK BASTARD

It's been a few weeks since Rebecca and I was humiliated at Alex's party. It didn't take long to spread throughout our town and the surrounding counties. Everywhere we go, there are sad looks or devilish smiles and whispers. Things at home have been pretty uncomfortable lately. Everyone seems distant and quiet. It's nowhere near the laughter that uses to flow through this house the last few years. It's been hard to look at Mr. Delruso, because you can see the anger in his face. It's difficult for him because there's really nothing he can do, we're all kids and that's all we've been hearing lately is that, "We are all kids."

There has been a ton of people stopping by to say how sorry they are including the parents of the kids involved but honestly, they didn't seem like they cared. They seemed a little afraid of Mr. Delruso, but most of them looked at my mother as if she deserved it. The blacks and whites would look and shake their heads. I guess in so many words there saying we should have known better. After all was said and done the truth came out about what happened.

Rumor was Joey and his friend Rob set things in motion the night of Alex's party. You see Alex had a huge thing for Joey which made it easy for him to convince her to turn against her own friend, Rebecca. Joey told Alex to convince Rebecca that Rob was interested in her, and wanted to talk to her so she did it. Rob made Rebecca a drink which he told her was Gatorade, but he left out the part about him slipping a roofie in it. They sent Amanda to keep me distracted while they colored Rebecca's face with a black marker as she sat passed out on the living room couch. Alex and Leslie grabbed her legs and Joey grabbed her shoulders then they carried her outside, but not until Rob pinned a sign to her dress that said, "Nigger Lover." They dumped her beside the house in Alex's mom's flower bed. They laughed and poured beer on her as the other kids looked on.

Joey and Rob convinced Alex, Amanda, and Leslie how cool it would be to have a great party story when they get to high school. Alex always had a need to fit in with the in the crowd, she was afraid that her social status would change now that she would only be a freshman. The word around town was she was saying, "Somebody has to be sacrificed for the greater good." Meaning she would sacrifice Rebecca so she could remain popular.

Rebecca and I walked through the fields and talked a lot the first few weeks of summer. I could tell they really did a number on her. I have been black all my life so it didn't really affect me as much as her. I'm used to the racism. I was more concerned about her getting through it. She looked at me one day as we were walking, "Bro, high school is going to be unbearable to us now isn't it?" she asked. I looked at her, "Naw it's going to be fine, the summer just started everyone will forget by the time we go back to school," I said.

I really knew that was a lie, but she was feeling so horrible I couldn't dare tell her the truth. Early Saturday morning I got up at day break and got dressed as if I was going to the field to pick berries. Mom, Mrs. Sharon, and Rebecca were getting ready to go to the market for food. I got on my bike and road towards the old neighborhood.

As usual Whiteboy Vegas was at the pond fishing, something he liked to do every Saturday morning. He said it helps him to remember his granddad. He was happy to see me like always, we shook hands and I could tell by the look he had on his face he had heard about what happened. "Are you ok Adrian, is your sister ok?" he asked. "We will be, I need a big favor dude," I said. "What?" he asked. "I need to use your old bike, the one with the broken chain, do you still have it?" "Yes," he replied. "Tell your mom someone stole it." When he heard that, he gave me the strangest look. "What if someone sees' you with it, you're going to get in trouble dude." he said with a really concerned look. "Just go get the bike and meet at my old house," I insisted. It didn't take long for Whiteboy Vegas to ride up on the bike we had built with old spare parts. It was old with rusty bicycle rims and painted with no gloss black spray paint. I left my bike at the old house and as I rode away Vegas shouted, "Don't forget, don't ride too fast the chain is going to pop off."

As I pulled out into the street I could see some of the elders standing in the middle of the road. As I got closer to them I could hear one of them ask, "Is that Azzy's boy?" The other one said, "Where is that little badass black bastard going?" I just spoke and continued to ride on until I came upon a broken tree branch on the side of the road. I pulled over, picked it up and broke it again to about the size of a baseball bat. When I looked back at the two men, they shouted, "Careful little man," as if they knew something was going to happen.

I rode the bike quickly back to the Delruso's home. I opened the barn in the back yard and put the bike inside. I grabbed some electrical tape and wrapped the broken stick from top to bottom. I ran inside and made sure no one was watching. I took the pliers from the drawer by the kitchen sink. Then I ran to my room and got my Syracuse Starter pullover hoodie. It was almost 12:30pm which was the usual time some of the high school kids would meet at the neighborhood park to play basketball.

I use to see Rob on his bike riding up the trail every weekend going to meet Joey at the courts. So I hopped on my bike and headed to the trail. I went over to the bench, flipped my bike upside down and waited on side of the trail with the hoodie covering my head. I pretended to be working on my bike. I took the pliers from my pocket and took a link out of the chain. With the chain off I wrapped one end of it around my right hand as the other end of it drug across the concrete. I was sweating because it was hot that summer morning. I kept glancing to the left patiently waiting for Rob to come speeding by on his bicycle as usual, and sure enough it didn't take long. From a distance, I could see him pedaling as fast as he could. His white Nike t-shirt was blowing in the wind. He had His backpack on speeding on his black silver and red sports bike. The closer he got the tighter I gripped the chain around my fist. I kneeled down beside my bike as if I was trying to tie my shoe. My heart was racing so fast I thought it would jump out of my chest. He's so close to me now I could hear the turning of his bicycle petals. Just as he was about to pass me I gripped the chain one last time spinning to the right and swung as hard as possible. I could feel the chain as it wrapped around his face, so I pulled back

68

with all the strength that I had. Blood shot across my orange and white

Nike Starter hoodie. The breeze was strong that day. When I looked down at him he was catching his breath from hitting the concrete so hard. His nose was flapping in the wind like a slice of wet bologna. I'm not sure what scared him more, the pure pain of the chain slashing through is flesh or the fact that I calmly put the chain back on the bicycle and casually rode away.

At a distance, I could still hear his screams of agonizing pain. At that point, I walked the bike into the woods where there was a pond. It had a lot of ducks and a sprinkler in the middle. I took my hoodie off, tied it around the frame of the bike and pushed it into the water. I ran fast as I could back to the Delruso's home with sweat pouring down my face. As I entered the back door, there stood Mr. Delruso at the kitchen sink, "Adrian, you OK?" he asked. "Yes sir, I'm just thirsty." I replied. I filled my cup with apple juice and noticed Mr. Delruso looking out the living room window due to all the sirens passing the house.

My adrenaline was pumping. I went to my room and paced back and forth a nervous wreck. Suddenly I thought, "I won't get a second chance to fix this," so I ran into the barn and got my taped up broken tree branch. I brought it back to the guest house. I went to the shed that Mr. Delruso kept his hunting gear and cut some string from one of the old bows in his archery collection. I took an old arrow that obviously hadn't been used in years. The tip of it slightly rusted. I tied the string to the stick until it bent in the middle making a homemade bow, something I learned playing with my friends in the old neighborhood, once the pressure on the string was perfect, I threw it across my shoulder making sure no one was looking and ran up to the street into the woods. I walked for about 20 minutes until I came up on the basketball court.

I quietly kneeled beside the tree and observed the kids playing basketball and sure enough, there was Joey, loud and arrogant as always. I took the arrow slid it into the bow and waited patiently. I didn't want to shoot wildly and risk hitting one of the other kids so I just watched. It paid off because suddenly arrogant Joey caught a fast break and couldn't help himself but to talk trash all the way down the court. As he ran, in the back of my head, all I could hear was, "ACL - ACL." I pulled back the arrow and as soon as he jumped to lay the ball up I released the arrow hitting him directly in his ACL. As he fell out the air he landed very hard, snapping his shin leaving it piercing through his skin. I could hear him as well and the other kids screaming. "Oh my God, look at that fucking spare rib!" one of the kids yelled out.

I ran back as fast as I could and broke the arrow apart, taking the string away from the stick and tossing it aside. I stuffed the string into my pocket, once I got to the street I started walking slowly as if nothing happened and continued back to the Delruso home. I went and took a shower, put on basketball shorts and a tee shirt, slid on my flip flops then sat on the front porch. Mr. Delruso was coming from the mailbox, he stopped in the driveway and gave me the strangest look as if he was thinking about something for a split second, and then he smiled and shook his head and walked in the house.

SEVEN

SHATTERED GLASS AND RED ROSES

Our small town is on fire. Over the past few months, a lot has happened. It's a bit much for the locals to handle. It's one thing when our evil deeds are kept quiet, but now that media is taking notice people are getting very uncomfortable. The attack on Joey and Rob got some of the parents in an uproar. That's putting a lot of pressure on the police, especially with the lawyers involved.

News cameras are everywhere trying to find out what happened. Rob spent the summer in and out of the hospital, he needed plastic surgery. Some of the kids at school have been gossiping, they say no one has seen him since the assault. It seems all the kids in our school imaginations have gone wild and the stories are becoming even more ridiculous by the day. Some say he is disfigured for the rest of his life. Some say he had plastic surgery and got an entirely new face.

Joey is walking again now, but he's still limping from his injury. They say it will be a while before it heals, but they doubt he will ever play college basketball now. They say his mom told Alex's mom that he tried to commit suicide twice already. Alex say's he just sits in his room all day and pops Percocet's. Other than school, he's not very social and even at school he's distant. He's definitely not the loud, arrogant Joey that everyone remembers.

There are rumors all around about what happened to them. Some of the parents are saying Rob and Joey were selling drugs, everyone knows that Joey's older brother is a heavy cocaine user. Some of his relatives are known to sell drugs and can be very violent. Rob's family are deeply involved with the Aryan Brotherhood, I use to see him with Whiteboy Vegas' older brother HardRain a lot. Everyone in town seems to be very concerned about these two boys. A whole lot more than they were worried about Rebecca's assault.

It seems like that "little" incident just faded away, at least to them it did. At home, it seemed like it stole all her joy. She went from wearing bright colors and being bubbly, to dark colors and being depressed. The Delruso's had kept her sheltered from how cruel the real world could be. Her first dose of reality may have just been more than she could handle. As we all started growing up, Rebecca being the princess of our town was becoming a battle between all the teenage girls and it became fierce.

High school was totally different; a bunch of heartless angry teenagers fighting for attention and some would do anything to get it. With Joey no longer being our high school's basketball star, Alex was no longer interested. She still succeeded in gaining popularity because even though she wasn't known as Joey's girlfriend, she was known for her party that humiliated Rebecca, and she was the girl who knew all the information about Joey. A lot of it was things she made up and the rest was the adult's imagination gone out of control and talking in front of their kids.

Alex and Rebecca went from best friends to worst enemies. Leslie was Alex's "do girl" and number one fan. Amanda was stuck between feeling guilty for what they had done to Rebecca and not wanting Alex's wrath turned towards her. Alex was quickly building a reputation as a hot chick not to be messed with. Even some of the upperclassman envied her. Most of the guys wanted her because she dated Joey and most the older girls had to include her in their activities because the older guys were into her.

The more Alex's popularity grew the more horrible she treated Rebecca. I hated it. They would knock her books out her hand on her way to class. They started leaving notes on her locker calling her a nigger lover and someone even said I hope you get raped by that ape. I had been going through this for years so I was kind of over it but Rebecca, I was starting to think wasn't going to be able to get over it that easy.

After school, she would get home and go straight to her room to cry. At dinner, you could tell she'd been crying, we all knew because her eyes would be blood red and puffy. My mom was getting worried, so she talked with Mrs. Sharon and asked her does she think it would be best if we left. Mrs. Sharon talked with Rebecca, and Rebecca just wasn't having it. Later that night Rebecca heard the sound of my basketball hitting the ground in the backyard and came outside. "Can I talk to you Adrian?" she asked. "Sure, what's wrong?" "I think I know what happened to Rob and Joey, you don't have to tell me anything if you don't want to but I promise I'll never tell a soul," she said. She paused and then asked, "Was it you, Adrian?" I held my head down and took a deep breath, my heart was pounding. I looked up at her, "How did you know, do you think the cops know?" I asked. "No, I went to your room to get my Super Mario game the day it happened; I saw blood on your shoe beside your bed. I wiped it off so nana wouldn't see it. I wish I was tough like you Adrian, Alex is making my life unbearable," she said. "You are you're my sister." "I love you bro," she replied smiling. Even though I never wanted her to look at me like I would hurt someone, it felt great to talk to her about it. I was driving myself crazy with worry.

I couldn't help but wonder if anyone knew I had done it. I thought Mr. Delruso knew, but he never talked to me about it so I wasn't sure, and I definitely was not going to be the one to bring it up. On top of my fear of going to the slammer, I felt terrible about hurting Rob and Joey. I probably shouldn't after how they treated Rebecca but I do. Sometimes I feel like if I had stayed in the old neighborhood none of this would have happened.

Well, tomorrow's Saturday and Rebecca and I are excited some of our friends from the old neighborhood are coming over for a cookout that the Delruso's are having. All summer Rebecca and I mostly hang out with them because our parents have been a bit skeptical about us being with the local kids after everything that's been happening. Vegas came over with Devon, and mom invited our next-door neighbor Mrs. Alice from our old neighborhood with her two twin daughters Suga and Moundoo. I'm guessing you can figure out which one loves soda. When Moundoo was a baby she loved the soda Mountain Dew but couldn't say it, so she called it Moundoo. They were a little rough around the edges but they loved Rebecca, they could Double Dutch for hours. Suga and Moundoo were a bit tomboyish and Rebecca loved it because growing up on a farm made her the same way.

A lot of the girls at our school always hated Rebecca for that, because she could always play with boys. Mrs. Sharon and Mom are allowing everyone to stay the night because tomorrow is Halloween, and after the cookout we all are in a rush to go to sleep and wake up in the morning. We spent most of the afternoon talking about our costumes and the Halloween parties that might be going on tonight.

As usual, Alex is having a party and almost the entire school will be there. We aren't allowed anywhere near there after what happened to Rebecca so Vegas, Devon and I are spending most of the night playing Nintendo and Sega. We're excited about all the candy we get to demolish tomorrow. Devon seems to be spending most of his night getting yelled at by Moundoo for sneaking in the fridge stealing and drinking all her "Mountain Dew." He's upset because for some reason she put a dozen of them in the icebox part of the refrigerator and they're frozen solid. A few hours later we were tired of playing Street Fighter nonstop on the Nintendo, Vegas is thirsty and decides to knock on Rebecca's door to ask for a soda but they ignore him and don't answer. So he decides he's just going to take one anyway only to open the fridge and see that the girls moved the frozen sodas. "Awe man, this suck," he yelled out. Devon and I laughed… All of a sudden, we heard loud banging on the door. Vegas ran to the living room window, "Halloween isn't until tomorrow stupid, oh shit!" he yelled out. "It's the cops," shouted Devon. Mr. Delruso answered the door, "Can I help you, officer?" I stood still, my body riddled with fear. I knew my life was over at that moment, I'm going to the big house for life. "Sorry to bother you this evening sir, we're in the neighborhood notifying parents that there has been an attack on a teenage girl at a Halloween party in the area so it would be a good idea to monitor your kids until we find out who's responsible," he said. "Oh my God what happened, who was it, are they OK?" asked Mrs. Delruso. "It was a teenage girl named Alex Monroe," the cop replied. "The

Mayor's daughter?" my mom asked, "Yes," the cop said. "All we know at the moment is three people with stocking caps over their faces and hooded sweatshirts on approached her at her party and threw frozen sodas at her striking her repeatedly in the face and head. It was horrific the way the onlookers described it. They picked the soda cans up off the ground when she fell they continued striking her. We had to rush her to the hospital," said the cop. "It was horrible," the other officer added. "She was holding a vase of roses the mayor sent to her when she was attacked, it was shattered right beside where we found her," he added. "Oh, my God, let me tell the girls to be careful," shouted Mrs. Sharon.

She ran to Rebecca's room and beat on the door. "Yes mom," yelled Rebecca as she opened it. "You girls make sure you're careful this weekend, that girl Alex from your school has been attacked," said Mrs. Delruso. "Oh, my God what happened?" Rebecca asked. "Someone bonged the shit out of her!" Whiteboy Vegas yelled. My mom shook her head in disbelief as she looked at Vegas, "That damn boy," she said.

EIGHT

ROSE GOLD CHARIOT

Christmas is in the air and I love it. The music is festive, the smell of fruit and sweets and most of all the happy people. Things have been good lately. Mr. and Mrs. Delruso are in the Christmas spirit, mom is laughing sharing memories of dad while she's cooking and Rebecca has finally found herself again. For once my entire family is happy and it's been so long since I've seen it this way.

We have two Christmas trees, one in the main house, and one in the guest house where mom and I live. Today

Mom and Mrs. Sharon are baking cookies while Mr. Delruso, Rebecca and I are putting the last touches on the tree. "Mom how did you and Nana become such close friends?" asked Rebecca. "Well, one day I said Azzy, I wonder why people always making such a big fuss over race, and she said to tell you the truth honey I don't know, the only difference between a white woman and a black woman is one got to sleep in the house, cause they both got beat when the master got drunk I've never quite heard it like that," said Mrs. Sharon. "Can ya'll not get them into that political revolution talk please," shouted Mr. Delruso.

All the adults laughed and then the Isley Brothers came on the radio singing a Christmas song. Mom and Mrs. Sharon started to scream how much they loved that song then grabbed Rebecca and I, and started to dance. Time is moving slower the closer Christmas gets and I can see all over mom's face that she got me exactly what I wanted. Every time I mention it she smiles and says, "Baby, I know you want that go cart but there just so dangerous and not to mention expensive."

I usually don't ask for things that pricey but I figured I'd give it a try this year. I'd even show mom how much I deserve it. With only three days left before Christmas, I have to get on the ball. Tuesday morning, I got up early grabbed my shoes, brushed my teeth and washed my face then out the door I went. I got the rake and went to work, and the yard was filled with leaves that morning. An hour passed and Mom came to the porch and shouted, "Adrian it's breakfast time!" "I'm not hungry I got tons of work to do today Mom," I replied. She smiled and shook her head as if she knew what I was up to. After breakfast, Mr. Delruso, Mrs. Sharon and Rebecca all came out and walked towards the car. "You sure you don't want to go to the mall with us Adrian?" asked Mrs. Sharon. "Come on

Adrian," Rebecca shouted. "I can't I got to rake the leaves," I said. Mr. and Mrs. Delruso laughed and shook their heads.

86

Everyone knows what I'm up to but I don't care that go cart is coming home to daddy. That afternoon came quick, I'm dusty and thirsty so I jog across the yard and enter the back door. "Hey mom, can I -" and those are all the words I got out before a man stepped into the kitchen grabbing my mom from behind and wrapping his left arm around her throat then began to choke her.

Another man ran from the living room into the kitchen striking me across my face with a silver revolver. I fell to the floor, my ears ringing loudly and blood gushing over my left eye. I yelled out in pain blinded by my own blood. "Shut the fuck up!" the men shouted. At this point, I could taste the blood in my mouth. I wiped the blood from my eyes with my shirt sleeve so I could see mom. I could hear her gasping and kicking from the man choking her. Every time she would try and scream he would punch her in the right side of her face really *hard*. Her eye was bloody and instantly swollen up. He pulled a syringe from his pocket and put it towards her neck. The other man grabbed me by the throat and screamed, "Look at her! Look at her nigger! If you say anything your nigger lovers are going to be next!" He stuck the needle in mom's neck. As soon as he released her they both ran for the front door. I ran as fast as I could towards mom hoping to stop her from hitting the floor, but I slipped in my own blood. I jammed my pinky finger trying to break my fall and keep my eyes on my mom at the same time. She hit her head extremely hard on the deep freezer as she fell to the floor. Her body jerked and trembled for a few seconds before I got to her. "Mom!" I screamed over and over as loud as I possibly could. I shook her shoulders and attempted to open her eyes, and then I ran to the phone and called 9-1-1. Being so shaken up I could barely talk, I told them the address and I sat beside my mom in shock and speechless, when I heard someone open the front door I froze in fear. I heard everyone screaming, but it was muffled due to the continuous ringing in my ear. My head was pounding;

the last thing I remember was Mrs. Sharon screaming my name.

That morning I woke up in the hospital. It seemed like everything on my body was numb. My left eye was bandaged, I was sure I had lost it and would never see out of it again. My left pinky finger was wrapped up, and the left side of my jaw was swollen. Rebecca sat to the right of me holding my hand, beside her was Mrs. Sharon and at the foot of the bed was Mr. Delruso. Everyone looked fuzzy, but I could hear Rebecca sniffling. "Adrian we're here honey," said Mrs. Sharon. It seems like the whole incident came flashing back. I began to cry uncontrollably, I had this sudden intense feeling of emptiness. I groaned loudly trying to fight back my tears. I rolled over towards the right where Rebecca was sitting, and put my face in the pillow and screamed out in agony. Rebecca grabbed me and pressed her face into my shoulder and cried out, "Nana is dead Adrian, and she had a heart attack." I turned back over hugged her and slid to the side so she could share the bed.

Mrs. Sharon's face was a bright red and her eyes were full of tears. Mr. Delruso held her closely as he wiped his eyes. The cops came in shortly after that and asked me a lot of questions, like, "What happened and did I see anything?" For a second I wanted to just tell them everything. I didn't care what happened to the people that killed my mother just as long as something happened. "Adrian, you don't have to be afraid, nobody can hurt you now," said the cop. I instantly remembered what the man said, "If you say anything, your Nigger lovers going to be next." I just lost my mom, there's no way I could lose Mr. Delruso, Mrs. Sharon and Rebecca too, so I hung my head and mumbled, "I heard something fall when I was outside raking the yard, so I ran in the house and mom was on the floor shaking." "So how did you get the gash on your eye and why is your face swollen," he asked? "I slipped in mom's blood when I ran to the phone to call for help," I replied. "What about your finger and the bruises on your mom's face?" he asked. "I don't know, I guess she hit it when she fell," I said. "Well I'm sorry for your loss kid, it seems your mom had a massive heart attack, I heard she was an amazing woman," he said.

I watched as he walked out the room and with him any chance of getting revenge for my mother's death. There were two men that killed my mother and just one of me. They came into our home, if we weren't safe there we weren't safe anywhere. Realizing there would be no payback was a hard pill to swallow. The Delruso's took me home that afternoon, Rebecca and I sat quietly in the back seat of the car. Things had changed, we had been through some pretty rough moments but this was different.

When we pulled into the driveway Rebecca hands began to shake and her eyes started to water, So did mine, to be honest, I fought back the tears and grabbed her by the hand and we slid out the left side door. The last thing I wanted was to go back inside this house but what choice did I have. When we walked in, it was a strong smell of bleach, almost blinding. Rebecca ran to her room and I sat on the couch with my eye bandaged up and my hospital band still on. As reality sat in that mom was gone the tears started to roll again. My heart was racing and my thoughts were dark.

I began to think what's going to happen to me now, mom was all I had. Mr. Delruso and Mrs. Sharon were in their bedroom so I stood up and walked towards the front door. Usually, I'd go through the back door to get to the guest house where Mom and I lived but I can't dare go into that kitchen right now. To be honest I'm scared, as I got closer to the guest house my eyes looked at each window. My mom just passed away and I'm alone, what if I see her ghost or what if those men come back? Mom no longer

works her so I guess I should leave now. I sat at the foot of my bed elbows on my knees and face in my palms, thinking about what I'm going to do while my eye throbbed from my injury.

I crawled up to my pillow and tried to rest my eyes for a second. I felt a hand on my shoulder shaking me, when I opened my eyes it was Mrs. Sharon and some strange lady. The room was filled with morning sunlight but a feeling of despair. The lady looked like she had brought bad news. She had long brown frizzy hair with hints of gray and pasty white skin. She attempted to smile but you could tell she was embarrassed by her smoke-stained teeth. She smelled of cheap cigarettes and yesterday's liquor. She didn't say too much, just wrote a lot and looked around. She sat at the edge of my bed and asked, "Adrian how are you doing?" I didn't say anything I just glanced at Mrs. Sharon. "Are you hungry?" she asked.

"No ma'am." "This is Jessica Reeves, she's from the Department of Social Services. She just wants to ask you a few questions." "Are you happy here?" the social worker asked. "Yes ma'am." I glanced at Mrs. Sharon with a confused look, wondering why the lady was asking me these questions. "Are you here to take me away?" I asked the social worker "Not today, we're trying to see what arrangements we can make for you." I looked back at Mrs. Sharon, "Don't worry Adrian, everything is going to be just fine," Mrs. Sharon assured me.

Over the next few days, my mind was all over the place. Between thinking I could end up living with some strangers or some group home, and my mom's funeral my whole world was out of balance. Mr. Delruso knocked on my door and brought in a black suit for me to wear to my mom's funeral. I stood up from my bed, looked at the suit and put my head down. Mr. Delruso gave me a hug and laid my suit on the bed. "Tomorrow's the day we lay Azzy to rest, I know this has been hard for you Adrian, it's been hard for us all," he said. "Do I have to go?" I asked. "As hard as this may be, yes you do. I wish I didn't have to go either. We all love Azzy and we all have to go pay our respects. When he walked out of the room I shut the bedroom door, fell against it, slowly sliding to the floor. I sat for a few minutes in a daze wishing this was a nightmare.

How did my life go wrong so suddenly? I got up and closed the blinds to the windows so the room could be dark. I turned off the television and the light, got under my blanket and attempted to sleep the entire day away. I tossed and turned all afternoon and all night long. In the wee hours of the morning, I drifted off to sleep to be awakened by the voices of the people gathering for my mother's funeral. I sat up in my tank top and gummy bear boxer shorts. I walked to the window and peeked out. I could see cars lining up down the street. The yard was full of a whole lot of people and most of them I never have seen before. I wondered how my mom knew all these people.

Mr. Delruso was standing right in front of my door. He turned and knocked on it. I opened it. He asked if I was getting ready. He said he'd send Rebecca over with my breakfast. I said OK, shut the door back; I was overwhelmed and exhausted because I didn't get any sleep. I went to take my shower. The hot water hitting my head and face woke me up. I brushed my teeth and looked in the mirror sadness covered my face. My eyes looked exactly how I felt, like a little boy that's lost everything. I put my suit on and sat on the bed. A few minutes later Rebecca knocked on the door. "Come in," I yelled. "Hey bro, I have your breakfast," she said. "I'm not hungry." "Me either, who are these people Adrian?" she asked. "I don't know, I don't really want to go." "Me either," she replied in agreement. "But we have to, it's Nana," She grabbed my hand and we walked out the door.

Everyone turned and looked at us. They knew what she meant to us Mrs. Sharon walked over, took us both by the hand and we all followed Mr. Delruso to the limousine. As we looked down the street it seemed as if there were black shiny Cadillac's for miles. The hearse was shiny and black also. I could see mom's casket through the back window. As everyone was getting in their car I walked up to the back of the hearse. Inside was an all-white casket trimmed in Rose Gold. Everything was so shiny, the gold, the cars, even the white on the casket. As I walked away to get inside the limo with the Delruso's, all I could think was how much it seemed like the hearse was a chariot and my mom was Queen for a day, at least that's how I preferred to remember it.

NINE

ME, MOMMA AND GOD

Its' been a long weekend, mama's funeral was not only one of the worst days of my life; it also left me with a lot of questions. Like where did all the people at her funeral come from? I've never seen half of them before. Most of them were dressed like rich people. I saw some people from my old neighborhood I hadn't seen in a while. It was good to see the familiar faces especially my friends Whiteboy Vegas and Devon. They sat about five rows behind us and I was really surprised Vegas' mom brought him. She doesn't care too much for blacks; at least that's what she makes her husband believe. Some say she's not so bad; she just does what she has to do to survive living with a racist husband.

There were a lot of fancy cars there with license plates from a lot of the different states. Mama never left Virginia so I found it interesting that these people knew who she was. Rebecca and I seemed to be lost in the crowd; we just stood to the side as Mr. Delruso and Mrs. Sharon talked and greeted the people. There were many people that approach them giving their condolences. Most of the men were in nice suits and had very cold faces. The women wore pretty dresses and most of them smelled of nice perfume and looked upset and exhausted. They smelled nice, but it was very strong and filled the church. Some of the elders from my old neighborhood were coughing with funny looks on their faces. The blacks and the whites honestly seemed like they thought they were better than one another. When I got back from the funeral I just sat in the guest house wrestling with my own thoughts.

The quiet was driving me crazy but I wasn't really in the mood to talk. It didn't seem like anyone else was either, everyone was quiet and distant.

No one could really believe mom wasn't there. Mrs. Sharon sat on the steps of the front porch looking out into the yard with her elbows on her knees rubbing her fingers through her hair. It was obvious she was broken, her closest and it seems her only friend is gone. We all could hear the banging of the hammer coming from the barn where Mr. Delruso intended to spend the remainder of his evening. It was just him a bottle of Jack Daniels and a bench he was pretending to work on. With all the banging, clanging and loud screaming of curse words, I don't think the bench will be much to sit on.

Rebecca attempted to sleep but couldn't help looking out her window multiple times to see if I was outside in the yard. Sometimes when I looked through my blinds at my window our eyes would meet and we would quickly back up.

Walking around the guest house was hard; everywhere I looked made me think about mama. Her church shoes were still beside the couch, her purse was still on the coffee table. Her white church gloves were by the front door on the shelf where we keep the mail. I picked them up and walked over to the couch, sat and started to cry until I heard a knock at the door. It was Mrs. Sharon and Mr. Delruso; they came in and sat down with me in the living room. "Adrian I'm so sorry," said Mrs. Sharon. I shook my head up and down as I quietly looked at the floor. "Adrian you're like my son," said Mr. Delruso as he started to break down and cry uncontrollably. I glanced at Mr. Delruso, stood up walked over and hugged him. "What he's trying to say Adrian is the social worker is coming back in the morning to ask you if you would like to live with us permanently, and we wanted to know how you felt about that because we don't want to lose you?" Mrs. Sharon asked with tears running down her cheeks. "I really want to stay," I replied while wiping my running nose and the tears from my eyes. Mr. Delruso and Mrs. Sharon grabbed me, hugged me tightly and exhaled. "Does Rebecca know?" I asked. "She's waiting on your answer now, she was afraid you might leave her so she didn't want to come out here, how about you go tell her your answer," said Mrs. Sharon.

I gladly darted out the door full of excitement with some great news that I really needed. I knocked at Rebecca's door, "Come in," she shouted. "Guess what?" I yelled. Rebecca looked at me with optimism as if she knew I had said yes I would stay, but also a hesitant look of I'm not too sure. "I'm staying forever!" "Cool, I knew you wouldn't leave us Adrian!" I smiled and we laughed for the first time since mom died.

That same evening, we all pitched in moving all my things into the main house. For the first time, I started having separation anxiety due to being away from my mom. Leaving the guest house was bittersweet. It was sweet because I wasn't going to be alone and bitter because Mom and I shared so many good times there. Over the next few weeks, I took my time and boxed up all of my mom's things. We just left all the boxes in the guest house and we took all the pictures to the main house. Mr. Delruso said we could store them there just in case I want mom's things when I'm older. Sometimes I sneak in there and look through her stuff when I'm missing her really bad, and that seems to be happening a lot.

I always wanted a brother or sister; I just wish it wasn't under these circumstances. I think this is the first-time Rebecca has lost someone close to her. It seems like Mrs. Sharon can't do anything right for her these days. It seems like everything she attempts to do Rebecca says, "Mom that's not how Nana does it." I can tell it frustrates her a little, after all taking care of people is what Mom did for a living and Mrs. Sharon misses my Mom just as much as Rebecca does. Everyone is handling it in their way I guess.

The school season came back around rather quick; all the parents are out shopping. I always loved this time of year it puts a bit of excitement in the air. Rebecca and I will be sophomores, the big tenth grade where you're old enough not to be a freshman but still young enough to get pulverized. Today is Tuesday and I'm at the shoe store hoping they have a pair of white and black British Knights left. We've been searching all day and I'm tired of shopping. Mom and Rebecca can do this all day but it's not really my thing.

Rebecca and I are older now, she's fourteen and I'm about to turn fifteen., so the looks that people give us in this town has gotten worse and bolder. We laugh because they look at us like we might be dating. Mrs. Sharon tells us not to pay them any mind but she laughs hysterically when I call her mom loudly and the onlookers stare and shake their head. I think the racist people that live in our town think it hurts our feeling but they don't know that we been dealing with this so long we learned to find humor in it.

Being so young when my parents died I found comfort over time in calling Mr. Delruso and Mrs. Sharon Mom and Dad. I knew they could never take the place of my real parents but it was nice to have that family structure. Besides I been around them so long it all seemed natural, at least till school let back in. Well, some things never change. Mrs. Sharon Dropped Rebecca and I off on the first day a school. To be honest we're not kids anymore so were aware that these assholes don't care too much for our blended family.

Everyone has their reason it seems or they're more than willing to create one. Most of the moms at our school think Mrs. Sharon is playing saint trying to save the poor black kid, the fathers think was the beginning of the jungle fever epidemic and the kids at school there just begging for an ass whipping. Rebecca and I aren't cute little kids anymore after the shit we've put up with from these people, where feeling pretty damn dangerous. As we stepped from

Mrs. Sharon's caravan and entered the school all eyes was on us but we didn't care. We entered the hallway with our heads held high. Rebecca wore a white mini skirt, red and white puma sneakers with a red Chicago Bull's jersey and an all-white Kangol hat. I wore a black tank top with white cargo shorts a black Los Angeles Raiders hat and black British Knight sneakers. Of course, they looked at us like we were watching too much Yo! MTV Raps" but the box cutter Moundoo and Suga gave Rebecca, and my screwdriver that I took from Mr. Delruso's tool box would beg to differ.

I've already thought about this, I'm willing to take responsibility for whatever might happen this year. Whatever my sister does I'm taking responsibility for that to because I've got her back. As we strolled down the hall we were glancing at the bystanders with our wish your ass would look on our face. For a second it felt so good I got afraid myself of what we might do. In the back of my head, I realized I better have a sit-down tonight when I get home between me, mama and God because if we don't get some divine intervention I think there might be a massacre brewing.

TEN

A DARK CROSSROAD

The first few weeks of school were fun, Rebecca and I went to every football game and every party other then you know who, "Alex". Whiteboy Vegas, Moundoo and Suga would always meet us there. Boy, we just loved to make an entrance. Rumors were all over the school that Rebecca may have attacked Alex but no one could prove it. Seeing her around town with two other girls didn't really help since the cops said it was three people who attacked Alex. The tables had turned; Alex was not such a bully anymore. Rebecca seemed to be coming out of her shell she had a social life now. She had friends, boys that wanted to be her friend, she had respect now and she was enjoying it.

At some point, I kind of wondered if my sister was enjoying it too much. I tried not to say anything because I knew she had gone through so much the past few years that she deserved to let her hair down. I also started to become a little concerned she was starting to get a bit aggressive. For a while it was like she was looking for a reason to hurt someone.

I think my final straw was when Rebecca skipped class one day to go to Carter High School and help Moundoo and Suga fight some girl who said Suga was ugly. That school was known for its reputation of fighting. It's the school I'd be going to if Mom and I hadn't moved. That entire day I walked around our school looking for my sister and she was nowhere to be found. I started to get worried; it's not like her to just avoid me. I asked a few people had they seen her but everyone seemed a little hush-hush. When lunch came around I was livid and began to approach things from a different angle, like somebody better tell me where the fuck my sister is. "Amanda" who I hated dearly approached me and said, "Rebecca is at Carter." I looked at her with my face frowned up and asked, "What the fuck is she doing there?" "I don't know," she replied. I was suddenly struck by panic and disbelief, why would she go there without me. What in the hell is at Carter that she needed? Then it hit me, Moundoo and Suga go to school there and if my sister had to hide the fact she was going there it couldn't be good.

I couldn't focus for the rest of the day all I could think about was every ridiculous way I could get to Carter. It was too far to walk but even if I tried to and Mrs. Sharon saw me Rebecca and I would be toast. My nerves were shot, for the rest of the afternoon only thing on my mind was what if my sister got hurt. The end of the day the last bell rang and I slowly walked out of class wondering what in the world was I going to tell Mrs. Sharon when she asks where Rebecca is.

As I was walking down the hallway I could see a girl skipping towards me. When she came into view, sure enough it was Rebecca. I stood still, speechless and angry as I stared at her. "What in the hell is your problem man?" I asked. "What Adrian, I had to go do something it was important," Rebecca replied. I shook my head and walked towards the exit to meet Mrs. Sharon. "You going to proud of me, I fought this girl today and won," said Rebecca as she giggled. I didn't respond I just kept walking. When the car pulled up I notice Mrs. Sharon wasn't driving, it was Mr. Delruso. "Hey dad," shouted Rebecca as she ran to the car.

When I got in the back-seat Mr. Delruso locked eyes with me in the rearview mirror. He looked at me like something was wrong I could tell he wasn't so happy. Rebecca carried on for five minutes about how her imaginary day in class went. "If you let one more lie come out of your mouth, I'm going to push you out of the car while I'm driving!" shouted Mr. Delruso. I dropped my head thinking oh my God she's caught. I looked up at Rebecca as she looked at her father like a deer in the head lights. As Rebecca started to stutter my heart started to race. "You have exactly thirty seconds to tell me what you were doing at another school, why were you fighting and do you know how much this is going to cost me to make this go away?" shouted Mr. Delruso.

Rebecca closed her eyes and put her head down and didn't say a word. "You girls really did a number on that kid," said Mr. Delruso. Which one of you had the box cutter?" he asked. "I don't know dad, I didn't see any box cutter," Rebecca replied. "Adrian, do you know anything about this?" "No sir," I said. When we got home Mrs. Sharon was standing on the front porch with a look on her face that would strike fear in Satan. "Come here, young lady," she said pointing at Rebecca. Sis turned and looked at me as if she wanted to scream Adrian help me. I walked into the house and as I went towards my bedroom I overheard Mrs. Sharon say, "I'm afraid Rebecca, I'm afraid that the direction you're going there's only one outcome for you and I don't want anyone calling me to tell me you're in jail or dead!" I stepped into my bedroom and slowly shut the door. I hate to say it but Mrs. Sharon is right and I also hate to admit that if it happens it would be my fault.

I know mom is rolling over in her grave at how Rebecca and I are behaving. What if something did happen to my sister I wouldn't be able to live with myself. This family has been so good to my mother and I. Rebecca was always nice and would never hurt anyone and now she seems like she's becoming just like me. I watched her change into this person and didn't do anything to stop it. I think it's time I grow up and do exactly like I promised to do and that is take responsibility for whatever my sister did wrong.

Life is funny sometimes how things work out. I'll be sixteen next year and my real dad left my grandparents' home at about my age. I'm nowhere near the man my father was but my dad and the men at Juke Joint always said I had heart. I guess it's time I prove it because if I stick around any longer Rebecca is just going to become more and more like me. I can't lose her, it would kill me and letting Mr. Delruso and Mrs. Sharon down would too. I went to my secret stash spot which was really just a reebok classic box in the back of my closet. I had been saving my allowance and birthday money for a while now. I had around twelve hundred dollars I think that's enough for me to move somewhere far away.

I could find me a job get an apartment and mom would be proud of me. "I got it! I shouted." "I'll go to New York City and become a rapper if I come back a star mama will be proud of me, and nobody will hate Rebecca and me anymore because I'll be famous." The only problem was I'm too young to buy a bus ticket, but I always been a pretty bright kid. I still have all Mom things and I've seen Mom call the bus station for Dad and buy his ticket over the phone to visit grandma. I found Moms purse and wondered if I pretended to be my Dad and say I was ordering a ticket for my son would they let me buy it. It's worth a try I thought, so I called and sure enough it was easy as can be. I gave them the numbers off mom's bank card and they didn't doubt me one bit.

I filled my backpack with a few clothes because there was no way Mrs. Sharon was going to just let me walk out of the house with a suite case. I waited until the middle of the night and quietly tiptoed right out the door. My bus leaves at six in the morning thank goodness the station is only about a mile up the street. I got on my bike and pushed it slowly out the driveway hoping my sister wasn't looking out the window. When I hit the street, I got on and peddled fast as I could until I was out of sight of the house.

When I got to the bus station I prepared myself for the hardest part of the plan which was retrieving my ticket. There's a possible chance that my brilliant plan is about to become unraveled. I walked up towards the ticket counter extremely nervous and it got worse when I saw the cop standing at the snack machine. There was an older gray-haired black man standing behind him and I'm hoping he stay there long enough to block his view. The lady at the counter called me next, I inhaled, walked up to her and said, "Adrian Delruso I'm here to pick up my ticket." "Identification please," she replied. My hand started to shake a bit as I passed her my learners permit. She glanced at my permit and sure enough, I knew it was coming, "Are you traveling with an adult?" she asked. I pointed directly at the nice old black man standing behind the cop and said, "Yes ma'am, with my Granddad." She printed my ticket and kindly replied, "I hope you have a nice trip sir, come again."

I sat by the window staring at all the faces of the people that were traveling that morning. When the doors on the bus shut and we began to pull off I looked around to see who was sitting next to me. This older lady and I made eye contact as she tried to quiet her screaming baby. My nervousness suddenly turns to a strong sadness and I wanted to go home but it was too late we had left the station. As I watched the lights shine through the bus window onto my face I remembered something my dad would say. There are only two types of people on the trail way bus and that's poor people and people leaving cause they sure not going. I never really paid it much attention and now I get it. We were leaving because something bad happened and were not just going because we can't afford a vacation. I just slid down in my seat and attempted to hide the flowing tears from the strangers that surrounded me.

ELEVEN

AMERICAN PROM QUEEN

Arriving in New York City for the first time was not exciting as I always thought it would be. I can see why they call it the big apple, everything is huge here. I can't lie I'm half afraid and half amazed. All the buildings and lights are mind blowing and there are people everywhere. I should be happy but I can't help it, I miss my family. I know by now there looking for me and I'm sure Rebecca is in an uproar. I hope they found the letter I left on the kitchen counter and perhaps they will understand why I had to leave. The letter read as follows:

"Dear Mom, Dad, and Sis, I know right about now you're very worried about me but don't be. I'm very grateful for everything you guys have done for me and my Mom. I'm so sorry that I had to leave, but it was time for me to grow up and be my own man. You guys have given me such a wonderful life and I don't know what I would have done without you. That is why I think it's only fair to let you enjoy the rest of your life without having to worry about the people in town staring at us everywhere we go. I want my sister to know what it feels like to not have to be defensive at school because she has a black brother. Dad, I want you to be able to do business around town without being penalized because you have a black son. Mom I would like you to be able to relax at the hair salon and not have to overhear the rude comments the other mothers make about me because I know it hurts your feelings. Things will be better this way so don't be sad everything will be fine. Yes, Mom, I have my coat, yes Dad I have some money I saved a lot of it, and yes sis I

119

can protect myself. I can't tell you guys where I'm going because I know you'll just find me and make me come home. Well, I have to go now I'll write soon.

Love always,

Adrian Delruso."

When I got off the bus at the Port Authority terminal in Downtown Manhattan I realized this bright idea I had was going to be much harder than it sounded in my head. It was very noisy and even though there were thousands of people it seems like they didn't even see one another everyone had tunnel vision. I walked out of the station onto the sidewalk and the noise got even louder. There were car horns, people yelling at one another and they even had a police officer on a horse. I couldn't help but wish Rebecca could see this, she loved horses so did Mrs. Sharon.

I clutched my backpack tightly as it hung on my right shoulder after all this is New York and I've heard some crazy stories about this place. I started walking down the street looking around hoping I can find a hotel. I try to stop a few people and ask but they kept walking. I'm a little hungry so I stopped at a food cart and ordered a hot dog and a soda. The man kept asking what kind of pop I wanted and I had to tell him several times, I just want a hot dog and a soda until I realized in New York they call soda's "pop".

The man was foreign so I could barely make out what he was saying but I decided to ask him where I could find a hotel. He asked how old I was and I told him fifteen he said no hotel would rent to me. I got a little irritated at that point, I was exhausted from my trip and I had a terrible headache I just wanted to go to sleep. He recommended a place in Harlem close Lenox Avenue I looked at him with confusion because I had no idea how to get there. You can only imagine how happy I was when the man offered to help me. He was getting off work in about thirty minutes and told me if I hung around he would show me where to go since he had to catch the subway that direction anyway.

The man was really nice he gave me two sodas and two bags of chips before we left. When his replacement showed up they shook hands, spoke in a foreign language and we left. When we went down into the subway it was one of the coolest things I ever saw. "You like that; you got any family in New York?" the man asked noticing the smile on my face. "No, I just moved here," I replied. "Oh ok, where you from?" "Virginia," "Oh cool, I got family down there I love Virginia," "I'm tired it's been a long trip," I said to the man as I yawned and stretched. "We here now, let's go, this our stop the man said. We got off the train on 145th street uptown Harlem and it looked nothing at all like downtown Manhattan. It was dark and there wasn't a white face in sight, only Spanish and blacks as far down the block as you could see. The noise was still the same but the smell was different. It changed from the smell of roasted peanuts and cotton candy to piss and marijuana.

"You smoke weed my man?" he asked. "No, not

lately anyway I've tried it once or twice," I said. It made me think about the day Vegas, Devon and I went fishing. Vegas had stolen some of his brother's weed and we smoked it at the pond. "Here you go," he said passing me a joint so I could take a hit. I took a few puffs and passed it back. We walked up to 148th and Fredrick Douglas where we saw a small park, it was more like a tennis court with a fence around it. "Hold on I got to take a break I'm an old man I can't keep up with you youngin', let's rest over here on this bench for a second," he said. We walked over and sat down on the bench as he continued to smoke his joint. I was starting to feel a little buzz from the weed actually more like I smoked a blueberry field full of weed. "Sit right here," he said. I sat down, and gladly because if I stood any longer I was going to fall. "So, are you planning on staying in Harlem for a while?" he asked while patting me on my knee. "Yes," I said uncomfortably. "Good," he replied while starting to massage my knee firmly. "Bitch, get the fuck off me!" I shouted as I jumped up. "Fuck you, I was trying to help you little man!" he screamed out. As I turned to walk away he hit me right behind the ear. I fell like a ton of bricks and rolled onto my back. The man was approaching me very quickly so I stood up, grabbed my backpack and reached for my knife. "Don't move little nigga!" he said as he pulled out a small black handgun. I knew I was in trouble when he pulled the gun, but I knew I was in big trouble when his foreign accent went away.

"Leave him alone!" a voice shouted. I sat there motionless not knowing what to do next. "I'm about to call the cops!" the voice said as it got closer. "Give me your money," the man demanded. I forked over all my money as the voice was starting to turn into a young girl about my age. "What are you doing to him?" she asked shouting at the man. He took my money and ran off into the darkness. I was left bleeding, scared and humiliated in front of this beautiful girl and that's not all because now I'm broke and homeless.

"Are you ok?" she asked. I shook my head yes but I wasn't, not even close. She took off one of her silk gloves and gave it to me to hold on my eye. I had hit my face on the pavement when I fell. I looked at the girl kind of strange because she was all dressed up and were in a dark park in the middle of the night. She was dressed in a pink and white dress with high heel shoes and long silk white gloves; she also had flowers in her hair. "Oh, its dance night and I was supposed to go but I got stood up. My foster mother is sort of an asshole so I just figured I'd walk around until the dance is over so she won't throw it in my face." "Oh, I see and I thought I was having a bad night," I replied as we both laughed. "Hi, I'm Noreen." "Hi I'm Adrian, Adrian Delruso." "Well nice to meet you Adrian Delruso." Even though I was pretty fucked in the rooming board and eating department, I think I'm starting to love New York City.

TWELVE

THERE'S A RAGE IN HARLEM

I slept outside last night, even though it's fall the nights in Harlem are cold. The weather gets cold but the hearts of some of its residents are frozen. I'm a long way from home and everywhere I look reminds me of that because nobody loves me here. I'm starving. I slept in a corner behind the Hamilton projects, on the dirty concrete balled up in the corner like a stray animal. My clothes are starting to look dingy and my tongue tastes terrible because my mouth is so dry. My good idea is getting worse by the moment. People are passing by eating breakfast as I stroll slowly up Fredrick Douglass Boulevard. I can smell food coming from the bodega on the corner where the weirdo robbed me.

I saw a homeless man in front of a drug store begging for money and the bottom of my heart fell out, "Oh my God that's going to be me." The day was starting to warm up and I would give my left arm for a glass of water right now. It's funny how we take the simplest things for granted when it's plentiful. My feet are hurting and so is my back. I think I'm going to die out here, I swear the sun is pressing down on my swollen eye. It hurt so bad that if I didn't know any better I would think God was trying to kill me.

I saw a dumpster in the corner behind one of the project buildings. There was a little bit of shade on the side of it so I stopped there to rest for a while. I saw a small black and brown dog; it came up to me so I played with it for a while to take my mind off how empty my stomach was. An old black lady was walking towards me with a large black trash bag she was bringing to the dumpster but it burst on her. I ran over to help her. "Thank you, such a nice young man," she said. I threw her trash in the dumpster and continued to play with the dog at least until he began to sniff around and walk towards a sweet potato that had fallen from the old lady's busted trash bag.

The dog looked back at me, then back at the potato. I got a little closer and noticed there was a piece missing from it. I looked over at the dog his ears stood up. I looked around to see if anyone was looking then looked back at the dog and clinched my teeth. It was apparent our bond was over. "Adrian!" someone called out. The voice was familiar, when I turned around it was Noreen. "Hi," I stood there embarrassed because I looked horrible and I hadn't had the best night.

Goodness, she was beautiful, such perfect skin so pretty smooth and brown it looked like melting chocolate.

Her eyes were very slanted almost like a cat and her teeth were white like a sheet of paper. She has a slight accent so I asked her where she was from, "Cameroon," she said. "Is that close by?" I asked. She laughed, "No silly it's in Africa." "Wow, what are you doing here?" "My Grandmother brought me here when I was nine; she passed away a year later so here I am." "Sorry," I said softly. "Do you miss it?" "I miss the peaceful Cameroon, but when I left it was far from peace." "Where are you from?" she asked. "Virginia." "Do you miss it?" "Yes, I do," I replied as I hung my head down. "So why are you here, I mean don't you have family there?" "My Mom and dad died a few years back," "I see, are you hungry?" she asked. "What makes you think I'm hungry?" I answered defensively wondering if she had seen me eyeing the dog's potato. "Because the bad man took all your money last night, you silly boy," she said as she chuckled. I shook my head in embarrassment but there was no way I could make it through the night with no food or water.

I didn't ask where we were going; I didn't really even care as long as there was food there. "You know I live with my foster mother, she's a demon bitch but no worries she's not there right now you just have to be gone before she gets home," said Noreen. I thought we would have to walk a long way but we didn't she lived in the building right beside the park. We went into the building and went towards the stairway.

"What floor do you live on?" "Six, but I take the stairs it keeps me in shape and besides these common ass niggas be pissing in the elevator." We ran up the stairs to Noreen's apartment. When we walked in there two other girls, one was Puerto Rican and the other was Korean. "I thought no one was here," I said. "These are my foster sisters they're cool, this Adrian y'all, and Adrian this is Sherry and Jackie Chan, I'm joking, this sister Lola we call her Lo," she said while bursting into laughter. "Jackie Chan wishes he was fucking Korean," said Lo.

The sisters vanished to their bedrooms while Noreen made me a plate of the leftovers Sherry had made earlier. It's was Cornbread, spaghetti, and green beans. It didn't take long either before it disappeared right off the plate. "Goodness Adrian you must have been hungry," said Noreen. "Thank you so much," I said with a shy laugh.

"Take your clothes off." I looked around in shock and confusion. "So, I can wash them silly, you can take a quick shower before the demon gets back!" she said laughing loudly. "Cool," I followed Noreen to the bathroom; she waited outside the door for me to pass her my clothes. While I showered, Noreen, Sherry and Lo packed me some food and water. Lo gave me some extra socks and Sherry gave me some hand towels. It was almost time for the demon to come home so I hugged Noreen and thanked her and her sisters for their help. Lo walked up to me and said, "Noreen is my sister, and I love her, she's never brought anyone here before so there must be something special about you. You got to be careful on the streets of Harlem. Life is hard here you have to fight to live, or life will kill you." She passed me a grocery bag with a balled-up bath towel inside. "Thank you and take care," I said as I graciously smiled on my way out the door.

I walked back over by the dumpster sat down and put my headphones on while I searched through my backpack to see what they had given me to eat. They had given me enough sandwiches and fruit to last me tonight and tomorrow night. Plus, I had face towels that I could wash up with in a public restroom. I picked up the Grocery bag that had the big towel I could use for a blanket. I pulled it out and unrolled it to see how long it was and out falls a small .22 caliber chrome pistol with a wood handle. I quickly scooped it up afraid that someone passing by might see it. I exhaled, it wasn't the best life but I felt a little bit safer knowing I had protection. The concrete was terrible; I tossed and turned all through the night.

When morning came, I could barely get off the ground my body was so stiff. I walked around that day trying to see what Harlem was like. I didn't want to wander off too far and couldn't find my way back so I tried to stay on 148th. I strolled up as far as Broadway and was in pure shock when I saw the Apollo Theater. I started thinking,
"Maybe things aren't as bad as they seem. Maybe the Apollo was a sign that I'm supposed to be here, maybe I can write me a rap song and perform at the Apollo," I thought. Right up until the weirdo who robbed me walked out of a bodega on Broadway. I ducked behind the people passing by with the worse thoughts going through my head.

I decided to shadow the weirdo for a few minutes to see where he was going. A few minutes went by and I looked up and seen the street sign say Lenox Avenue. "Got you bitch," I said. There were cops on almost every corner but I didn't care the more I thought about me sleeping outside cold and hungry I just wanted to release some anger. "Faggot motherfucker," I said as my eyes stayed glued to the weirdo. "I just can't believe this sissy ass dude embarrassed me in front of Noreen!" At that moment, I stopped in my tracks, "If I kill this queer I'll never see the girl who saved my life again," I thought as I stared at the man. I stood there and just watched with rage pouring out of my eyes and ears as the weirdo walked into his apartment building.

THIRTEEN

A FRIEND OF A FRIEND

Harlem seems unusually quiet tonight. It's been two day's since I've seen Noreen. The temperature is dropping again and my nose is starting to run. I'm wishing I was in the south right now so I could light a fire to stay warm. I'm grateful for this towel but it just doesn't seem to be enough right now. It's starting to sprinkle out here and I'm praying it doesn't come down hard. I can hear sirens speeding towards me. You can see all the lights headed this direction. I'm praying this weather holds up because if not they're going to be coming for me next.

There's a lot of commotion starting to come from Noreen's building. There's some guy coming out screaming at an older woman. I just looked on in shock because down south, parents don't play that. There's a girl running up the sidewalk knocking people out of the way. I really want to be nosey because I'm bored but where I come from there are consequences for that sort of thing so I'm not really trying to have a part in it, of course, I didn't want to but then the girl got close enough that I could see it was Lo.

"Go get Noreen Adrian!" she screamed as she ran by. "Where is she?" I shouted. "She's at the apartment with that fucking demon!" Lo yelled. I ran as fast as I could, you know misery loves company and the people were starting to gather. I noticed Noreen on the side of the building with some girls crying so I yelled her name. She ran over to me and grabbed me by the hand, "Come on," she shouted.

We ran up the block the same direction Lo was heading. "What the hell is going on?" I asked. We stopped running when we got to an empty store front. It looked like it had burned down and was under construction. Noreen took me to the side of the building and when we walked in. I saw Lo sitting on a bucket in the corner crying. She didn't really look like the Lo I met a few days ago. She looked extremely tired and she kept nodding off. Noreen was trying to keep her awake but she just seemed like she really needed sleep. Noreen called me over and asked me to help get Lo over to a mattress that was lying beside the wall. We covered her up and walked to the other side of the room.

"Are you going to tell me what's going on or what?" I asked. "The last few days Lo hasn't been feeling too good," she said. She looked at me and began to cry, I reached into my backpack and pulled out one of the hand towels they gave me and handed it to her. "Well our foster mother, the demon has a son," she started to explain. He's been raping Sherry and Lo since they first got placed with the demon. His name is Ty, he's probably one of the scariest people I ever met," said Noreen. "Have you told the demon what's going on?" I asked. "We tried, but she's terrified of him. He beats on his own mom and when he beats on her, she beats on us." "What kind of sick shit is this?!" I said. "Tonight, he tried to get me, Lo and Sherry helped me fight him off. Sherry stabbed him, the cops probably arrested her by now. It was pretty bad," said Noreen. "They need to be arresting his ass!" I shouted.

We could hear someone creeping around outside and we're getting a little nervous. It's probably the police because Noreen's shirt is full of blood. She grabbed my arm and moved closer to me. "Noreen!" someone shouted. "I'm scared Adrian," she whispered. I didn't say anything but honestly, I was scared to. "Noreen, is you in here I need to talk to you!?" they started shouting louder. At this point, I'm sure it's the police because it's a man and his voice is deep and scary like when the police are knocking at your door. "It's the police," I whispered to Noreen. "Oh, my God we're going to jail, what am I supposed to do Adrian?" asked

Noreen as she began to sob. "We just going to have to tell them the truth, that asshole tried to rape you and that he been raping Lo and Sherry forever," I said.

"We can't fucking do that, what if they put us in jail for stabbing Ty, Sherry not that sick yet but Lo is. She would die in there the fucking health care sucks!" shouted Noreen. "What's wrong with them?" I asked. "Ty has aids, Adrian!" "Fuck!" I shouted. "Sherry has HIV but Lo has full blown aids now. That's why Sherry stabbed him! They didn't want him to get me too. When Lo dies, somebody got to tell her story so that Social Services won't place any more girls in that home," she said. "Stay right here," I whispered. "What are you doing?" asked a panicking Noreen. "I got to go talk to the cops, at this point we don't have a choice there's no way out maybe they will listen to me," I said.

I walked out from behind a pile of wood that Noreen and I were hiding behind. It was dark and chilly. I could see Lo's silhouette lying on the dirty mattress beside the wall.

The noisy door slowly opened and I could hear the cop calling for Noreen. I tip toed towards a dark corner so he couldn't see me. He was a pretty big guy I could tell from the little beams of moonlight hitting him through the broken store front windows. He was getting closer, and then he got so close I could see this was no cop at all. He had on blue jeans, a bloody white t-shirt and he looked like he was in bad need of a bath and a shave.

My heart started racing because if it wasn't the police here to save us than it was Ty here to murder us. I came out the darkness and started quietly tip toeing behind Ty. He was sweating heavy and breathing very hard, the problem was Noreen was also. I could hear her breathing heavy and sniffling as she was moving around so Ty had to hear her too. It was bad, I could feel it, and I could also see it. Also, if I could see Lo on the floor from where I was standing you could bet Ty could too.

It was about to go down, I could tell because when Ty got right in front of the light that was coming through the window he had the worst devilish grin on his face. "Noreen, come here gal ain't going hurtcha, I just wanna talk to ya," Ty whispered. "Just go away Ty!" shouted a sobbing Noreen. "You know I love you doncha," whispered Ty. "Love done fucked you over bro," I said as I pulled the trigger (Bong). Noreen screamed from the gunshot, Lo was too weak to say a word. I'm from the country so I learned a long time ago the dark can be your friend or it can kill you.

Unfortunately for Ty city life never taught him anything about hunting because he walked to loud. Noreen came from behind the wood and looked at Ty on the floor bleeding from the back of his head. She gave me a funny look; like she was surprised I had it in me to kill Ty. She was shaken and far from ok, pretty much in shock. She looked at his body and then ran over to Lo wondering was she ok.

When Noreen turned her over on her back she had saliva running down her chin. She was so weak she could barely lift her arm. "This is the safest I've felt in a long time," Lo said softly. She had a slight smile but you could clearly tell she needs her rest so Noreen and I covered her up with the large towel they gave me. We sat at the foot of the mattress and Noreen curled up next to me to keep warm. "Do you know any Shirley Caesar songs?" I asked.

"Boy what you know about some Shirley?" asked Noreen. She buried her head into my shoulder and began to sing that old apple tree by Shirley Caesar.

I sat quietly admiring her voice with tears rolling down my cheeks. All I could think is we only kids, why us? The night went by slowly and we were freezing. That morning Noreen and I stood up stretching our aching bodies thanks to the concrete floor. "Lo, we gotta go," said Noreen. I looked over at Ty's body lying stiffly on the floor. I could tell Noreen wasn't even trying to look in that direction. She kept her attention on gathering the things they had left around the store front the previous times they had been there because it's obvious they can never come back. She reached down and grabbed Lo by the shoulder to wake her but when she turned her over she was blue as a smurf. I watched Noreen as she fell to her knees quietly and then put her face between Lo's neck and shoulder, she screamed so loud we should have been worried about someone calling the cops but we didn't care. Lo was dead, and so was a part of Noreen. We walked out the building that morning with a new understanding of how cold life can really be. After all, we had no other choice but leave our dead friend's body in the same room as her rapist.

FOURTEEN

SHE'S NEVER GOING BACK

The demon went to work this morning, it's the perfect time for Noreen and me to get some of her things and freshen up. Walking into that apartment just felt all wrong, it had the worst energy. I didn't know what in the hell we were going to do. First it was just me I had to worry about but now both of us are on the street. I needed to do something I just didn't have a clue what.

The weirdo had taken all my money, plus we were homeless and hungry. I started to think maybe I could call mom and dad, maybe they could come get us. I just wasn't sure they would allow Noreen to come knowing we were so young. I searched the apartment to see what I could find, maybe Ty left something of value around. In his closet, I found an all-black 9mm pistol and in one of his New Balance sneakers. I also found a bag of weed and some coke. I covered my hand with my sleeve and picked up the gun because Ty didn't seem too bright.

Overhearing my family and friends talk about it so much down home it was second nature to know what it was and what to do with it as far as the coke. I continued to search the room and found a scale in the vent with about

800$ in cash. On top the television was Ty's pager and wallet. Inside were his ID, insurance card, and a bank card. In the back of his wallet was our get out of hell free card, it was a phone number and under it said, "good shit". I chuckled, the irony, the same asshole I had to kill is going to be the one to save our lives. It's such a cold fucking world.

Noreen looked over at me when I laughed; she clearly wasn't in a laughing mood. I had to tell her something my father always uses to say. I walked up to her kissed her on the cheek. "Sometimes you don't want to do the things you're asked but you're going to do what you're told," I said. "What do you need me to do?" asked Noreen.

"I'm going to call this number from the demons' house because I'm sure whoever "good shit" is he knows Ty phone number. Tell him to meet you at the park by 8th and 145th. It's right behind the bodega. You gotta act like you're concerned about him so tell him there's a firehouse right on that street and cops be walking by, it will take away most of his suspicion." "What if he asks me what time?" "Tell him 10:00 pm." "I'm going to do this, but only if you promise never to ask me to be involved with anything like this ever again." "Scouts honor," I replied.

One thing the south always taught me is when you're hunting, if you blend in you'll always eat. We gathered

Noreen's things which weren't much but a few pieces of clothes and hygiene items. We took a trash bag full of food too, I didn't really want too, I figured that didn't belong to us but Noreen said Lo had bought it with her food stamps so fuck it, I hope the demon starve.

As we walked up the sidewalk we got a few stares because the whole neighborhood knew that pervert Ty tried to rape Noreen. A lady named Vivian walked up to Noreen, "Sherry wanted me to let you know she loves you and that she's ok, they locked her up," she said. "Tell her I'm going come see her soon as I can," Noreen replied as her eyes filled with tears.

We walk to a rundown motel up towards Spanish Harlem. I was hoping they would rent us a room. Noreen said they didn't care as long as you had money they would rent to pretty much anyone. She stood outside while I went in and tried to secure a room. I went to the counter and asked for three nights. "$198 and your I.D. please?" said the clerk. I reach into my pocket and pulled out the money and Ty's I.D. while hoping the clerk wouldn't have us sleeping on the street tonight. He looked at the I.D. then glanced back at me, "That will be an extra 20 dollars please." I smiled and gave him the money then went outside and got Noreen.

"Come on babe, let's get some rest," I said she looked at me, smiled and we went inside. The motel is a real shithole but compared to cold nights on dirty concrete it's a penthouse. There's only one bathroom on this floor and we all share it. I knew a hot shower was going to do wonders so I let Noreen go first. I sat against the wall outside the door while she was in the bathroom to make sure no creepies tried to get in while she was in the shower. I was so tired. I kept trying to rest my eyes. About a minute into her shower she screamed, it was almost like a painful groan. A couple that was walking down the hallway stopped and looked back at me like something was wrong. "It's been a fucked up few days," I said as I looked up at them. "Harlem," they replied as they shook their heads.

When Noreen came out the bathroom I folded the covers back for her to lay down and I covered her up. I went to take my shower and it was amazing. As it hit the top of my head and ran down my face I felt as if I was getting baptized and God was washing all of my sins away from the last few days. When I finished my shower, I went into the room grabbed a pillow and stretched out on the floor at the side of the bed Noreen was on. "Adrian cut it out, you been sleeping on the ground the last few days but not tonight," said Noreen. I got up and sat on the bed and slid beneath the warm covers.

Noreen laid her head on my chest and wrapped my arm around her. "Tell me about you, who is Noreen?" I asked. "Well, I was born in Cameroon it's in Africa. I had a sister, a mother, and a father; I had such a great family. We were happy, I loved my country. One day hundreds of young

149

girls just started vanishing. There were rumors in the village that the rebels were kidnapping the girls to sell as slaves and to sex traffickers, some they even kept as their wives," said Noreen. "Damn isn't that shit illegal?" I asked. "America has laws but some parts of Africa are lawless," Noreen replied. I understood that more than she knew because the small southern town I was born in was outlaw territory too. "Is that why you left Africa?" I asked. "Yes, I didn't really want to go at first. I mean where on earth could you find such beauty?" asked Noreen as she sat up in the bed. "I mean, Mother Nature has blessed Africa. You'd love it Adrian, the exotic animals are fit for royalty. The oceans, rivers and streams!" shouted Noreen as she jumped up and began to twirl like a young pre-school girl. I slid from beneath the covers up onto the headboard and tuned in to her conversation like it was an emergency alert radio broadcast. "The children would sing songs and it would sound like heaven's choir," she said. "The elders would speak to the village on Sunday morning and it would sound like God himself had sent down his holy messenger to bring his word. Then one morning my sister and mother went to the river and they never came back. My father went searching for them and he never came back either that's when I realized that this time someone had brought the devil. We waited for days but they never returned. All through the village people were starting to discuss leaving because there was talk that the Rebels would be coming, perhaps in a week or two. My Grandmother tried to tell the men in the village that the Rebels were already here but because she was a woman they brushed her off. So, my grandmother packed up what we could and we walked and walked and walked, I was sure we would die before we got to an American Embassy but we made it. A few days after being there our counselor told us our entire village had been slaughtered. Not long after that they sent us to

America and the whole plane ride I couldn't help but feel guilty. I thought about all my friends and family that had died and what they probably went through. When we got to America they put us in a homeless shelter for a month until they could find appropriate housing. We stayed in that shelter almost a year and it seemed more like a prison than a shelter for the needy. Right before Thanksgiving, my Grandmother went to take a shower and she never came back. The Counselor at the shelter came and told me she had a Heart attack in the shower and had died. Everybody always leaves me Adrian, I don't have nobody," said Noreen. "You have me and I'm never going to leave you," I told her. "What if I have to live with the demon again I have nowhere else to go?" Noreen asked as she sat on the bed and started to cry. "Look at me! You never going back" I said.

FIFTEEN

SOUTHERN SAVAGE

I remember overhearing Mr. Delruso talking to a man that came to our farm once. I was picking blueberries; at least I was pretending to pick them. The man looked kind of suspect to me and after seeing what happened to my real dad I just didn't like stranger dangers around my family. As they walked through the rows of blueberries I just thought I'd inspect the trees that they were passing. Mr. Delruso told him, "A man will do a lot of things he doesn't think he would do when it comes to the well-being of his family, even becoming savage if necessary."

Noreen and I had talked all that night. I didn't really get any sleep because all I could think about was when this money runs out so will our luck. I got up that morning and kissed Noreen on her forehead then hurried out. Today Harlem and I are going to have to come to an understanding. It was barely day lighting out, and Noreen was sleeping so good I didn't want to wake her. So everything I have to do needs to be done in a timely manner because if she wakes up and gets dressed she might come looking for me.

I didn't need much, just two sticks and believe it or not those are pretty hard to find in Harlem. I walked around the neighborhood for a while and there was no stick and no woods to run into. After I got frustrated I went up to a guy standing outside a bodega, "You know where I can find some trees?" I asked. "Yea, what you need I got twenties and dimes," he said. "Naw cuz, real trees, trees that grow out the dam ground." "These are real trees; these trees do grow out the ground little nigga!" he said with a confused look on his face. I just shook my head and walked off, "Fucking New Yorkers."

After looking everywhere, I got lucky there was a couple in front of me they were talking to a friend of theirs telling them they were heading to Central Park and that's just where I need to be so I shadowed them. We jumped on the train it didn't take long. When we got to the park it was huge and it had a lot of trees. I started looking for dried out sticks that was dead but not rotten. The first few I found had knots in them they were useless. I found one that someone had cut off but it was still way to green that's when I realize that the park groundskeepers must have been trimming so there has to be a pile of branches somewhere.

Central Park is huge so I figured if I find the trucks, and find the chainsaw sound ill find the sticks. It didn't take long, there was huge pile right beside the gate with plenty to pick from. I asked the Groundskeeper that was there where could I find a sporting goods store that I could buy fishing supplies in and he pointed me in the direction of one nearby. I walked a few blocks went inside and bought some fishing line and a hook. I got a nice hook to it had the orange and white bobber with a feather attached to it. I asked the clerk what train to catch back to Harlem and I was on my way.

When I got back to the block, I stopped and got two sausage egg and cheese bagels and two orange juices from the bodega. I also got Noreen a big frozen icy, the purple one. When I got back to the motel room she was just getting up and was happy to see me. I passed her the bag with the sandwiches she took it jumped on the bed, "What you got me?" she asked. We ate while she sat Indian style on the bed watching All My Children. I hated soap operas so I grabbed my stick and fishing line and got to work. "Babe what you are doing with that stick, going fishing?" asked Noreen. "Yea babe." "You just a straight up country boy, aren't you?" "Better believe it always and forever babe, can you help me with something?" I asked. "Sure babe." "Take this fishing line I'm going to cut three pieces off of it, I'm going to tie a knot at the bottom then I want you to braid it all the way to the top and I'll tie another knot in it." "Anything for Babe," she said.

We relaxed the rest of the day I kept noticing her eyes on the clock as it got later. "Adrian, I don't think you should meet that guy I got a bad feeling." "It's going to be fine," I replied. She kept looking at me like she wanted to ask me what I was going to do, but I think she didn't because she didn't really want the answer. About 9:00pm I got up and put my shoes on Noreen sat up on the bed with her arms around her knees. She wouldn't look up; I put my sticks in the corner. I grabbed Noreen in the head lock and kissed her on the top of her head trying to cheer her up. She didn't say much I picked up my backpack and walked out the door.

When I hit the corner of the block I saw a guy in a blue and white Fubu t-shirt. He was standing there bouncing on his tip toes looking around like he was paranoid. I surveyed the surroundings, there were a few people walking around and the garage door to the firehouse was closed. There is not an easy way or safe way to talk to this guy. I put my hat on and bought a newspaper from the Bodega.

I approached the park casually walking reading my newspaper. The backpack I had on and looking 130 pounds soak and wet made me appear as an innocent school kid. I entered the gate that wrapped around the basketball court. The man was standing beside the same bench the weirdo took my money on. I strolled over and sat on the bench. "Are you Ty's homeboy?" I asked quietly. "Who wants to know?" he replied calmly. "Friend of a friend," I answered. I let down the folded newspaper that I was reading and quickly pulled Ty's black 9mm from the middle. I raised it, (Bong)! I fired into his right temple and his lifeless body fell like a bag of wet sand. I noticed the lump in his right pocket I figured that must be the coke. I grabbed the bag from his pocket and ran off between the buildings that were covered in darkness and disappeared.

I took off the shirt I had on and switched it with one in my backpack. I took off the baseball gloves and put them in my bag as well. I took the bag and through it in the dumpster then I walked a few blocks and got my nerves together. I walked back to the motel and when I opened the door Noreen jumped right in my arms. "What's wrong with my babe?" I asked. "Shut up," she said as she hit me and laughed. "You hungry I made us some food?" "Gotta run out really quick babe, I won't be long I promise." I put the gun in a grocery bag and put it in the drawer. I got my sticks and braided fishing line, "I'll be back babe," I said as I kissed Noreen on the cheek. People had known the weirdo had robbed some kid at the park in Harlem.

The ass whipping he gave me, I might be able to deal with that. I come from the country we win and lose fights all the time it's just what we do, we fight. Like my Biological father use to say if you won every fight you just haven't fought anybody. Taking my money that's different and if I let it slide me trying to hustle in Harlem just might not go well for Noreen and me. I need to put enough fear in Harlem that there will be legends about me long after my death.

I walked over to Lenox Ave. I knew where the weirdo would be. He always at the same spot around this time a sandwich shop called Little Italy's. New Yorkers always had this fear of Italians but unfortunately for them, I'm from the south and we don't give a fuck about no guinea. I walked right up to the sandwich shop, went in and sat down right in front of weirdo. It was crowded but I didn't care I figured anybody who would eat with weirdo had to be dirty. He looked me in the face with a very shocked look, "what the fuck do you want kid?!" he asked. "I want my fucking money back!" I shouted. People started looking and laughing at weirdo making jokes. There was one fat Italian man behind the counter, "You took little man lunch money?" he asked, he wants his money back," he said as he was laughing really loud.

"It might sound funny to you sir but I don't see shit funny about a grown ass man trying to rape me, and when he couldn't he beat me up, pulled out a gun and took all the money I have left in the world," I responded while staring directly in his eyes. The fat guy stopped laughing and gave weirdo a mean look and shook his head. The rest of the men kept cracking jokes and the lady in the corner asked did I want something to eat. My blood started boiling, as they laughed I put one of my sticks between my feet to hold it sturdy while some Spanish looking man in a suit came out and called weirdo in the back.

They all stopped paying me any attention they were telling one another stories about how much of a bad ass weirdo was and bringing up all the horrible shit he use to do in the Bronx. The fat guy behind the counter stood still looking at me strongly wondering what I was doing. I took the first knot at the end of my braided fishing line and put between the slit in my stick wrapped it and tied it tight. Then I flipped it and did the same thing. I tapped the tip of my finger on the top of my other stick that I had burned and sharpened to a perfect point. I put my hands beneath the table and waited.

It was only a few seconds until weirdo entered from the back of the deli, "This little mother fucker still here?!" he shouted. Everyone got quiet and stared at me afraid of what weirdo was about to do. I noticed one thing that night; New Yorkers love to talk because nobody noticed except one man that I was putting a homemade bow and arrow together right in front of them. Within seconds of weirdo's remarks, my arrow struck his eye socket. I've never heard the words (what the fuck) mentioned so many times in sixty seconds.

Three of the men drew their guns, I knew I was dead when they started shutting the doors and closing the blinds. The Spanish looking man from the back walked in,

"You really needed that money didn't you kid?" he asked.

"It's been a fucked up few days," I said. "That's what I been hearing, put the bow down kid you safe here. I'm Malcolm, this shop belongs to me, but this your war so you get the spoils. Whatever he got on him belongs to you," he said. I looked around nervously; some of the people were horrified looking at weirdo with an arrow through his face. I cautiously walked over to weirdo and kneeled down and searched his pockets. There were a few hundred dollars in a rubber band, it wasn't twelve hundred though. There were some keys and a lighter. I stood back up and look at the man, "the watch and the necklace, it's all yours too," he said. I reached down and took the watch off his wrist and the necklace from his neck. "Those keys, they go to apartment 7b it's upstairs. I charge nine hundred dollars a month be here tomorrow at five we can talk business. Now get your little crazy ass out my shop so we can clean up your mess," he said.

SIXTEEN

SOUTH BOUND

Funny how time flies it's been 20 years now since I been in New York and it hasn't been easy. It was a rough start but things had gotten better. Norey and I got us an apartment right off Lenox. I had found work doing odd jobs for a big-time drug dealer named Malcolm. Our first ten years we had a good run but we were getting too much money so the Irish tried to muscle Malcolm but he wouldn't break. The Irish sent one of their replaceable do-boys to approach Malcolm after a basketball game at Rucker Park.

It didn't work out well for him the Irish new Malcolm had a bad temper; he beat the Irishman to death right on the sidewalk. It was lots of people there but nobody would talk so Malcolm's lawyer got him to take a plea for ten years. He probably could have beaten the charge but he didn't want the Feds sniffing through his paperwork, nobody likes that Rico law.

I got married, Norey is pregnant now, I think we are having a daughter and I'm happy but I can't say that it's honestly the best time for it. Norey is in school to become a Registered Nurse and she only has a week or two left. I'm detailing cars now and ten years ago you couldn't have convinced me this would be my future. It doesn't help that once niggas see you in your glory they won't let you forget how you "use" to shine especially these city niggas. Norey is a beautiful woman I'll be a fool to think they don't come at her, they just know she's loyal. They also know them odd jobs I do, I'm pretty damn good at them. It's been a struggle lately these fucking bills piling up. Norey try and keep a smile but I know she stressed and that isn't good for the baby.

Since she been pregnant I have been thinking about getting back out there on the streets but I think officer friendly done sniffed me out on one of them odd jobs because there's been a creepy ass white man following me around for the last few weeks. I told Norey about it and she just loves to go into a whole sermon about that's why I shouldn't get back out there. I can't lie though Norey is right about a lot of things, well almost everything. I'm looking at her right now sitting on the couch rubbing her stomach. She is smiling crunching on a cucumber as if it was the best thing ever. I can't really blame her because it's the only thing in there. I don't get my extremely small paycheck until next Friday and Norey food stamps don't come until Saturday.

Watching her so pleasant and happy knowing its Tuesday is kind of pissing me off. "What are you looking for?" asked Noreen. "Nothing important baby, just trying to find what I did with my calculator," I replied. Honestly, I was looking for my scale. I hadn't seen it in years so there's no telling where it is or if it's still here. Norey threw a lot of stuff away when Malcolm got locked up. She just doesn't trust anybody. I can't ask her has she seen it because she going to hit the roof and I might be in divorce court. I got to find it or go borrow one because we're not going to just be hungry. We going to be in the dark also, Norey had to call and get us an extension yesterday but they only gave us two days. At least they said they gave us two days because it looks and sounds like the lights just went off.

"What the fuck, I thought you called them people!" I shouted. "I did Adrian, they said they were going to give us till Thursday!" shouted Norey. I plopped down on the couch leaned my head back and put my hands over my face. "I don't know what the fuck we going to do now," I said. "It's going to be ok Adrian, God's going to make a way he always does," Norey Replied. "You're right, I'll be back in a little bit I love you," I said. "What are you about to do Adrian, don't do nothing stupid!" Noreen shouted. I grabbed my sweat rag and headed downstairs.

The sun was beaming so hot you could fry an egg on the sidewalk. I was on a mission and Norey knew me best because I'm about to do everything stupid. For the last few years, I have been trying to do everything right. I left the streets; I worked my ass off at a job I absolutely hate. I applied for almost every job in this fucking city it seems. I'm blinded by my own sweat it's so damned hot out here and I'm about to do whatever it takes to get them light's back on for my wife and daughter.

Right now, I just feel like I could push this whole fucking city into the Hudson. When I thought it couldn't get any worse, from the corner of my eye I could see creepy. This time creepy got some courage and he looks like he is approaching me. "Excuse me, excuse me sir are you Adrian Delruso?" he asked. My heart dropped but I kept walking.

All I could hear in my head was Norey crying. Damn, we spent the last couple of years struggling and they still took me down. "Can I just get one minute of your time sir?" he asked. "Creepy motherfuckers get killed around here you know that right?" I asked. "It's about your father," he said. I stopped and looked at him, "What the fuck you know about my father?" I shouted. "He's not well, he sent me to find you and ask you to come home," he replied. "You been watching me all this time and you just telling me this?" I asked. I looked at the man with tears in my eyes, "Is he ok?" I whispered. "I think you just better come home," he said. "Ok," I'll be there," I replied.

I walked back as fast as I could with the worst thoughts imaginable in my mind. When I walked in the apartment the lights were on and Norey ran up to me super excited. "See Adrian, I told you God would make a way!" "Did God make a way or did someone else make a way, don't make me fuck nobody up Noreen that shit goes for you too!"

I shouted. "Adrian, stop you know I would never, the lights just came back on and look, I went to the mailbox and this envelope was in there with our names on it. There's a lot of money in here. Do you know where it came from?" Norey asked with concern.

"There's something I got to tell you, come here and sit down." Norey walked over with a scared look on her face and sat beside me on the couch. "My father is sick, very sick and I have to go home." "You told me your parents were dead Adrian." "I know what I told you, and my biological parents are dead but I was adopted after my mom died." "Wow, and why didn't you tell me this I thought we shared everything?" "In the south things are different, a lot of people couldn't or just didn't want to understand my parents and sister adopting a poor black kid. They made life hard for my family and it was starting to have an effect on them so I left." "That still doesn't answer why you wouldn't tell me you have a family Adrian," Norey said with tears in her eyes. "You may have wanted to meet them and they're wonderful people. Also, we were young when we met, they could have made me come back home and I wasn't leaving without you." "We can talk about this later, right now we just need to figure out how we going to get you down to Virginia. That old truck gonna need some work, Adrian," said Norey.

I could tell she wasn't that happy with me but I think in a way she kind of understood. I had a pretty good idea how the lights got back on and where the money came from. I was just glad that Norey and the baby didn't have to sit in the dark or even worse the blistering heat. I took the truck to a mechanic up the street and got a tune up and some tires. It was 3,500 dollars in the envelope and that was enough to get the truck fixed, buy grocery and leave Norey some pocket money. I cleaned out the truck, got on I95 and headed home for the first time in over 20 years.

SEVENTEEN

UNITED NATIONS

Pulling back into town was bittersweet. A lot of the scenery has changed in 20 years. It brought back a flood of memories, some good and some bad. The old church is still the same from what I can see as I passed by. I see Reverend Moore is still there, he was moving a little slower around the church yard but he there. Some things do look a little rougher than I remember it but then again, I heard our generation was a little wilder than the one before us. I see that the corner store winos have slowly transitioned into crackheads. At least the ones that are still out there. I'm guessing old age

done sat the rest of them down and put a few on that grassy

hill.

I'm headed to that grassy hill now to visit the graves

of my biological mother and father. Walking up to their

grave site was tough. It looked like someone has been

keeping it up. There are flowers that couldn't be any more

than a week old. The collard greens that are planted right

next to all my family members are blooming very nicely. I

blew a kiss to my deceased family members and held my

head low because I knew they had been watching over me

for a long time now. I'm pretty sure my behavior hasn't been

in line with what they wanted for me.

"Mom, Dad, I'm sorry I really am. I'm sure these last

few years haven't made you too proud. I'm not really sure if

you're too proud of how I left this town or not but it's a call I

had to make. Mr. Delruso is sick Mom, and I'm about to head

over there as soon as I leave here. I don't know how bad it is, but a man came all the way to New York to find me so it might not be too good. Thanks Dad, even though I know you wanted better for me, the things you taught me is the reason why I'm standing in front of you today. Well, I'll be back to see you soon and this time it won't take twenty years. Oh, yea, I left that street life mom but there's one more thing I have to do. Those men that killed you, I'm going to take them fishing and have a nice talk with them about their behavior. I love you and dad, see you soon.

I got in my old pickup truck that was surely a rust bucket, and sounded like I had a monster in the muffler. The exhaust was so raggedy. I didn't mind though, I loved her. They used to complain in Harlem about her, especially when I was making good money. Didn't matter to me because I could see her future I was going to restore her to her former glory. When I pulled on the street we lived on and saw the sign Delruso Lane my heart started pounding and I smiled a little.

I wondered will they recognize me after twenty years. I've gotten a little taller and a little wider. Between Norey and the Spanish, they plumped me right up. Now Norey nags me every day because the doctor complaining about my blood pressure. When I try to tell her it's due to her good cooking she goes into complete denial. As I slowly drove down the lane it was if nothing had changed it looked like it was frozen in time. It was the end of the day so the workers in the blueberry fields were knocking off for the day.

I got out the truck and grabbed my duffle bag off the back. There was some old black man who stopped and looked at me, "I'll be damn if isn't Adrian Delruso, I'm glad to see you son, things just might be alright after all," he said. I glanced at him and continued towards the front door. I walked into the house and there was no one in the living room or the kitchen. I stood still for a second staring at the spot my momma laid on the night she died. I heard voices coming from Mom and Dad's room.

As I approached their door it sounded like an angry woman, "You have to focus on getting better dad," she said. Then I heard another voice that sounded like an older lady. "Is there anything I can get you honey to help you ease the pain?" she asked. Then I heard the voice of an old man, he coughed badly, "The only thing I need is my son," he replied. "It's been twenty years' dad, we have to start facing the fact that Adrian may never come back. He could be anywhere; he could be in jail somewhere or worse. You ever thought maybe he found his real family and just want nothing to do with us?" said the girl as she began to cry. "Rebecca, don't ever say things like that!" The lady shouted. "But it's true mom!" "Just pass me your father's medicine," said the old woman. At that point, I knew it was my family so I swung the door open, looked at Rebecca and said, "Now is that how you feel about your older brother?" Her mouth dropped to the floor, "Oh my God it's Adrian!" she screamed. Mom held her hands over her mouth and started to cry she was so surprised. "I knew if we kept praying you would come home," cried out Mrs. Sharon. They hugged me really tight and I looked over at dad. He had tears running down his face but he was too weak to move. I walked over and kneeled beside his bed. "I'm home Dad," I whispered. "Yes, you are son," he whispered through the rattling mucus in his throat. Rebecca excused herself so Mom, Dad and I could have some privacy. We talked about thirty minutes and I could see it was hard for Dad to keep his eyes open because of the medicine. I hugged mom and dad then told them we could finish our conversation tomorrow.

I picked up my duffle bag and carried it into my old bedroom where things were exactly the way I left them, well cleaner than I left it of course. I went into the kitchen and made something to drink. I walked into the living room to look around at all the old pictures. It brought back a lot of good memories. Through the window, I could see sis sitting on the front lawn smoking a cigarette. I walked out onto the front porch, "Got room for one more out here?" "Always bro!" I grabbed a chair off the front porch and walked over to Rebecca and sat down. "Dad's not looking too good, what's going on?" I asked. "The old man made us promise if you came home that he would get to be the one to tell you," Rebecca replied. I stood up and took a step towards the house. "He made mom promise the same thing so you're about to waste your time." I sat back down, "I thought that was a cigarette you were smoking," I said. "It is, it's a magic blueberry cigarette I'm smoking," said Rebecca as she laughed while passing it to me. I inhaled and it was probably the best-tasting weed I ever had. "Damn, that's some good weed." "Yea it is, a lot of things has changed around here bro." "It sure looks the same." "Well believe me it's not."

"Why did you leave bro, I needed you?" Rebecca asked as she tried to hold back her tears. "Honestly sis, I just got tired of the people in this town fucking with y'all just because y'all loved me. It became too painful to watch, they were willing to hurt you because you had a black brother. Mom lost all her friends and poor dad I was sure he was going to jail one day because of the people around here constantly attacking us. Most of all I didn't want y'all to get hurt because of me." "They may have said horrible things but they weren't going to physically hurt us," Rebecca replied. "Yea, just like they didn't at Alex's party." "Fuck her she's a little coke whore now," said Rebecca. "Well, just like they didn't hurt mom then," I said angrily. "How did they hurt Nana, Adrian, Nana died of a heart attack you know that."

"Hmmm, that's what they told us sis because we were kids but don't forget I was there." "Remember that kid Joey, he had some grown ass man with him when they broke into the house that day you Mrs. Sharon and Mr. Delruso went Christmas shopping. When I went into the house to get a drink of water I guess they were hiding in the living room.

179

Mom was sweeping the floor when I asked for some water. They ran into the kitchen and the man grabbed Mom around her throat and started choking her. She was kicking trying to get free, but he started punching her in the face with his free hand. Joey hit me across the face with a gun that's how my eye really got messed up. Joey pointed the gun at me and the man started screaming, "Do it, do it, clean that niggers fucking clock." The man pulled a syringe from his coat pocket and stuck it in mom's neck and let her go. When she fell, she hit her head on the deep freezer, blood shot everywhere so they panicked and ran. Knowing what I know now there must have been heroin in that needle. That's why it showed mom had a massive heart attack. They never thought to do a drug screening because everybody new mom would never do something like that." "What the fuck Adrian, why didn't you tell dad?" Rebecca screamed. "Because they said if I said anything my nigger loving family would be next."

EIGHTEEN

RAINING DOWN GUINEAS

I slept in a little late this morning. Nothing ever feels better than sleeping in your childhood bed. I freshened up then walked into the kitchen. My breakfast was on the table wrapped in plastic, just how I liked it as a kid, corn beef hash, cheese eggs, grits, and sausage. Mama didn't forget my favorite either, pancakes with homemade blueberry syrup. My fork was digging in that plate so hard I thought it would crack down the middle. When I was done, I walked over to the sink to wash my plate. I looked through the kitchen window and saw the workers on the farm laughing and talking with dad. Mom stood behind him pushing his wheelchair. I heard the screen door slam and I giggled a bit because sure enough, it was sis. My mom Azzy, use to get on her about letting that door slam like that. "What's up bro, how did you sleep?" "Like a baby," I said. "Dad said he wants to see you when you get a chance." "Ok, where you are going with your cowboy boots on?" "I got a date tonight." "Anybody, I know?" "Maybe but then maybe not, you don't have to worry though he's a real stiff." "Mom and dad meet him yet?" I asked. "Stop worrying I'm a big girl now. I'm going to pick up a few things while I'm out, do you need anything?" "Nope just for you to lose the cowgirl boots." "Whatever bro, don't tell me them city folks got you wearing mink coats and hats," replied Rebecca laughing loudly. "Only if I killed it," I said as I walked towards the door.

When I walked up to dad, mom grabbed me and hugged me tightly, "I'm so glad we're all back together," she said. "Me too mom it's good to be back." "Honey, give Adrian and me a minute," said Mr. Delruso. "Sure thing darling, if you boys need anything just give me a holler." "How about you take the old man on a little stroll son?" said Mr. Delruso. "Yes sir, dad I just wanna say I'm sorry for leaving the way I did." "It's ok son, I'm just glad you're here now."

I started to push dad slowly through the rows of blueberries. "Rebecca told me about the conversation you two had," said Mr. Delruso. "Really, and what exactly did she tell you?" I asked. I started to get a little nervous because I didn't want Rebecca to ruin what I had planned for Joey and his friend. "She told me about you wanting to protect the family. It was courageous what you did but it was foolish too, you were a kid you could've got hurt. Your mother and I knew what we were signing up for when we adopted you.

We knew these assholes in this town wouldn't make it easy for us. That's why it's hard for me to say what I'm about to say next, I'm dying son." "Dad this family is tough we've had our share of tough fights can't no doctor tell us when we going to die," I replied. "Son, just shut up and stop talking foolish come here and look at me," he said. I walked from behind the wheelchair and looked Dad in the face. "My cancer is stage 4 and its terminal. As much as I love you guys, and believe me, I've tried everything this world has to offer, it's getting hot keep pushing."

I got really quiet, so quiet I think dad could hear my heart breaking. He started trying to comfort me by talking about old times but I was zoned out and I just went deaf. "Adrian!" dad shouted. "Sir?" "Are you listening to me son?" "Sorry dad I was out of it for a second." "I was asking you have you ever wondered how our family got all the things we have?" "Not really dad, you just always worked hard." "Son, you ever heard of the Mafia?" Of course I have Dad, I was living in that hell hole called New York, how you know about it way down here is the question," I said as I started to laugh.

"I'm the leader of the Delruso Mafia Family." "Dad, it's getting a little hot out here maybe we should head back," I said with concern. Mr. Delruso struggled up from his wheelchair and as I grabbed his arm to help him, "Let me go!" he shouted. He stood up and slowly started taking steps forward with his cane. "I understand how this sounds to you son because we always tried to teach you and your sister to stay away from trouble and study hard in school. Lord knows Azzy probably would turn in her grave if she knew I was telling you this. Your dad though, I hate to say it but he was right. He always said you had that protector's instinct that most gangsters have." "I didn't know you knew my real father," I said. "Of course I did, I know everyone and everything about this town. He was one of the greatest men I knew. Remember the man you and your father shot at the

185

tracks across town?" "I shot one of them and how do you know about that. Dad promised we would never mention it again," I said. "Well, your dad shot the other one and then called me. I picked up the bodies cut them apart and buried them right up under them blueberry trees right there," he said. "Is that why you always use tell me and Rebecca those trees had worms?" I asked. "Yes!" "So dad, that means you work with some pretty dangerous people. If something was to happen to you God forbid, where would that leave the family?" "You're going to take my place." "WOW! Dad, if you think we had problems with these local Rednecks, I couldn't even imagine the problems we going to have with the mafia, that's a death sentence to all of us, Dad." "It's a death sentence to you, your mother and sister regardless if you don't step into my shoe's son. The New York Mafia's most dangerous family is run by Paul Puccini and he's one mean son of a bitch. The Puccini family is looking to go legal and they've wanted to get their feet planted down here for a long time I just wouldn't let him. If I die there going to try and take everything you, your mother and sister have." "So, you're telling me you would go to war over a bunch of blueberries?" I asked.

"Not just blueberries son but commodities and you'll find that it's much larger than that. Blueberries are used for more than just your mother's blueberry syrup son. A lot of foods require blueberries, just look at it this way, there are thousands of food stores and restaurants in New York imagine if you could supply them all with blueberries. Not only that, shipping blueberries require trucks but so does cocaine, marijuana, liquor, and guns," said Mr. Delruso. "Dad, what makes you think I can handle something like this?" "Like I said, I know everyone and everything that happens in this town. It took a lot of searching to find you, but when I did my people asked questions to make sure it was you. When I got the answers back I knew because you were strong as a kid and you're strong as a man. There's only one thing I want you to know, all I ever saw when I looked at you was my son, but all they ever going to see is your skin color. They're going to come after you and everyone you love. You can't show these people any mercy or they're going to take it as weakness. Before you let them destroy this family you burn this whole damn town down with it. You're not going to be able to do this alone. If you have any friends you can trust, this will be a good time to call them. Always be honest with your soldiers about the risk involved because they have families of their own. Just always watch and don't trust anyone. If they're not a part of your family assume they can always be part of your enemies' family. You always had a good heart but there's a day coming to where you just going have to put that shit under lock and key for a while. Always remember what you won't do to survive the next person will. "Is there anything else that I need Dad?" I asked. "A shotgun and an umbrella, because it's about to rain down Guineas," he replied.

NINETEEN

ROYALS AND REBELS

After thinking about what dad said I realized how right he was. I was going to need some soldiers and some that I could trust. It's still sinking in that my adopted father was mobbed up and I didn't know it. My real dad wasn't really as much of a surprise because now that I think about it, you could kind of tell he was about that life. I was a bit suspicious about all the strange people at my biological Mom's funeral. I thought about it for years, even though the Mafia would have been the furthest thing from my mind.

Trust comes hard for me; it's only been Norey and I for years.

I asked Rebecca was Whiteboy Vegas still around.

She said he hangs out in uptown Newport News right off Warwick by the shoe store Redface Rick use to own. He was one of the rednecks who got rich off the Marijuana rush. His dad was a tobacco farmer, so Redface Rick knew how to grow shit and he grew some of the best weed around.

I cruised around for a few hours enjoying the sites and looking for Vegas. I was about to give up because it was getting dark and I was getting hungry. Soon as I hit the blinker to turn right there Vegas was coming out the convenient store packing a fresh box of Newport's. I parked and hopped out the truck, "My nigga, my nigga," I said as I walked up to Vegas with my arms open wide. "What the fuck?!" shouted Vegas. He ran jumped on me hugging me as if I was back from the dead. It was good to see Vegas it's been a while since I knew anyone I could truly call my friend.

I had a hard life and Vegas knew it all from day one. We started walking down the alley beside the store headed towards where Vegas parked his car. "Where the hell you been man?" asked Vegas. "Shit dawg I had to return some favors so I moved to New York," I replied. "What kind of favors you owed in NY at fifteen years old homie?" "The favors I owed were here, you know my family was going through a lot of bullshit for adopting me," I said. As Vegas and I were walking we were clueless of the man following us in the blue jeans and Perry Ellis blazer. We were catching up on old times. "Did you hear about that punk ass Kevin Sullivan, he had Rebecca in his car and tried to get a little too friendly even though she told him to stop. I found her walking down the dirt road coming from the old fishing hole. I picked her up and she told me what happened. The bastard left her there because she wouldn't put out," he said. "Oh yea, wait till I see this motherfucker." "Don't worry about it

191

homie, I saw his ass at a party that following weekend I tried to beat his ass to fucking death."

Bong! "What the fuck?!" shouted Vegas. We ducked low to the ground our ears ringing from the gunshot echoing. When I looked up I couldn't believe my eyes. It was Norey standing there shaking with a gun in her hand. "What the fuck are you doing?!" I shouted. "That man was about to shoot you in the fucking head!" Norey screamed. I was in such shock thinking Norey had just shot me; I hadn't seen the man lying dead right in front of me. Blood was pouring from his skull like spilled milk. "Can we talk about this later we got to get the fuck out of here!" shouted Vegas. I grabbed Norey by the hand and we all ran to Vegas' car, jumped in and sped off.

Vegas was speeding and trying to light a cigarette but his hands were shaking too bad. "Slow the fuck down you going to get us knocked off by the law!" I shouted.

Norey sat speechless in the back seat, she was clearly in shock. We went to a hotel where I went in and booked a room. I came back out to get Norey and told Vegas I'll get up with him later but he refused. "I'll be right here outside keeping watch bro take your time," he said pulling a .45 pistol from under his seat. "That's what's up," I said as Norey and I walked into the hotel.

As we entered the room Norey slammed the door behind us "You got five seconds to tell me what in the hell is going on or I'm walking out that door and I'm never coming back!" she shouted. "Long version or short version," I said. "I'll take the short version please!" "My dad is dying, he has stage four cancer. My dad is the leader of a powerful Mafia family down here. He wants me to take his place but the Italian families in New York seem to want me dead." "Why, Adrian, did you do something?" "Yea, I was born black." "Fuck this shit, fuck this, fuck this, fuck this we have a family of our own to worry about Adrian!" "They're part of that family Norey, can you handle that?" I shouted. Noreen plopped down on the bed and put her hand on her stomach, "Oh my God I just murdered a man," she cried. "No, you just protected your husband from the man who was about to murder him," I said. "You were there for me when my life was hell. They tried to rape me; they tried to break me down and called me ugly with every other horrible name I can think of. I could've easily died in that apartment when we were kids but you saved my life. So I'm with you Adrian Delruso no matter what, if they're your family then they're my family too. You going to need an army Adrian," said Norey. I hugged her tightly, kissed her and whispered in her ear, "Get some rest I'll be back." "Where are you going," she asked. "I'm going to build us that army."

I went back downstairs where Vegas sat waiting in the parking lot. He gets out of the car and opens the passenger door for me, "Where to Boss?" he asked. "What the fuck are you doing," I said. I wasn't really in the mood for Vegas sarcastic shit. We got in the car and drove off. "The rumors are true aren't they Adrian?" "Depends on what the rumors are, you know 95% of the rumors in this town be lies," I said. "That your black ass about to become King?" I got quiet and stared out the dark tint on Vegas' window. "I'm gonna need some help dawg." "I'll be a motherfucker it is true!" shouted Vegas. "Is anyone still around?" I asked. "Pretty much everybody, it's hard to get your foot out this country pile of shit." "Where's Jackieboy and Devon these days? "Well Devon is a half of fag, I mean I'm not sure but he's a little different from when we were kids so I wouldn't count on him. That Jackieboy he alright I guess, you might have to feel that one out on your own. I do know my brother and your dad been doing some serious business over the last few years. You know me and my brother don't really see eye to eye, but with the type of shit you're in I'll talk to him if you want," said Vegas. "Fuckin HardRain, haven't thought about that racist asshole in years. He didn't even like us being friends when we were kids and now you think a country cracker going to help us kill a city cracker. Guess what the common denominator is?" I asked. Crazy ass Vegas started singing, "its raining crackers." We laughed, I told Vegas to round up who he could and I'll do the same then meet me in the barn behind Dad's house at midnight.

I picked up my truck and called to check on Norey. She was fine, happy to hear from me and that I was ok. In the meantime, Rebecca was on her date, she had drunk a little too much Jack Daniels. She pulled up to his mobile home and stepped out of her Ford F-150 screaming his name. "Joey, Joooooey, Joooooey!" she shouted with a country twang. She had a bottle of jack in one hand and a Marlboro cigarette in the other. Joey nervously peeked out the window, "Who the hell that is on my lawn?!" he asked. "It's me Joey, Rebecca!" Joey came to the door drunk, high off coke and confused. Rebecca wouldn't give him a chance in all these years and now to his surprise she parked on his lawn at

11:00pm drunk out her mind. "Rebecca, what do I owe the pleasure," he said slurring his words. Rebecca staggered closer and took a pull of her cigarette "I just came to give you some of this good ole' redneck pussy." Joey looked puzzled, "Well hell come on in why dontcha." Rebecca staggered into the mobile home trailer that was overrun by porn magazines and old car parts. On the coffee table lay a scale and a pile of coke. The trailer smelled like weed and throw up. "Feel free to have a little candy." "I'd love to, but only after the man of the house." Joey sat down on the couch in front of Rebecca and made two lines of cocaine and leaned down to take one. "Joey, do you remember my Nana?" "Yea, that old nigger maid y'all had, right?" "I asked Mama once how her and Nana became best friends, and Mama said Nana told her because ain't no difference between a white woman and a black women except one get to sleep in the house, cause master beat'em both when he drunk and mad, I think she was right." She pulled a small pistol from the spine of

197

her waist and pointed, "Joey did you kill my Nana?" asked Rebecca. He put his hands up but before he could speak (Bong!) Rebecca shot him right between the eyes. Joey's head fail face first into his pile of coke as Rebecca stood up taking a drink from her bottle of Jack Daniels and walked out the door.

When I pulled into the driveway I could see the living room light was on. When I walked in dad was still up watching the news and drinking coffee. I went over and sat on the floor beside his favorite chair. "They tried to murder me tonight dad," I said. "I know son, how's your wife?" he asked. "You knew I was married?" "Yes son, I figured you wanted to introduce her at a time that was comfortable for you. I got to say though, you should bring her here I think she would be a lot safer. There's going to be a meeting tomorrow I'm having lunch with Paul Puccini and I'm introducing you as my replacement wear something nice kid ok?" "Noreen got blood on her hands tonight dad; she had to murder that man to save my life. I could've been dead."

"Do you see how far they're willing to go? The next time it could be your wife, your mother or your sister. Now you go and you put your Gore-Tex boot so far up their New York ass that they taste deer shit for eternal life," said Dad.

My phone rang it was Vegas they were out back in the barn. I walked to my bedroom and grabbed my pistol. I went out the back door and walked past several cars and trucks that led to the barn. I walked in and Vegas pulled out my chair for me to sit down. I looked around the room and saw a few familiar faces and a few strange ones. There was Jackieboy; he was cool when we were kids just a little cocky. This older cat we use to call Big Bail because he was black as a car tire and worked in the hay fields since he came out his mother so he could lift the back of a Buick by himself. There were some men in the back I couldn't really make out because of the long hair and bushy beards but they had on blue jeans and flannel shirts. One had on blue jeans and a wife beater. I couldn't believe my eyes when I looked over in the corner; it was Suga and Moundoo. Everyone was talking except the men in the back they didn't seem to want to be there. A hand touched my shoulder from behind me and when I turned around it was Norey and Rebecca. Dad had called my sister and sent her to pick up my wife from the hotel. I didn't really want Norey to see this part of me because even though she knows me, she's never had to see it. I worked hard to keep it away from her.

I stood up from my chair, "If all of you are done making a friend there are a few things I think you should know before you agree to become part of this family. People may come after you, as well as your mothers, fathers, children and siblings. Your family members that have legal jobs they could be affected. These people can touch and perhaps destroy every part of your life. So, if this is something you can't handle at this moment you're free to walk out that door," I said. "Adrian, you know I'm with you dawg I'm down for whatever, but I'm not working with that redneck trash back there," said Jackieboy. "Then you're free to go." Jackieboy stood up brushed off his leather jacket and walked towards me heading for the door. Bong! I stood up and pulled my pistol from my waist and shot Jackieboy in his forehead. His body fell against the barn wall and slid down leaving a trail of blood. "Now does anybody else have a problem with the skin color of my uncultured friends?" I asked. No one spoke; from the back of the dark room the long haired white men approached lead by the bald headed one in the wife beater smoking a cigarette. "The names HardRain, I knew your father a long time, he was good to us. Them there Yankees would've been taken over everything but your father was always fair, and did everything he could to kept'em outta of here. When the old man is gone it's gonna get hard to feed our families with them city boys moving in. I'm sorry about your father and I like how you handle your business. I'll go to war with you any day Adrian Delruso," he said. I shook hands with HardRain that night, the man who was one of the most feared leaders of the Aryan Brotherhood.

TWENTY

WELCOME TO MY ZOO

I woke up this morning, looked over and kissed Norey on the forehead. I rubbed her stomach and talked to the baby for a second as Norey laughed and rubbed my head. I took a shower and started to get dressed for the meeting I had to go to with dad today. "If I knew you looked this handsome in a suit I would've been let you join the Mafia," said Norey as she laughed. I walked over to her and sat beside her. "We don't ever talk about that, I just work hard," I laughed and kissed her lips. Norey stood up and started helping get my tie right. "Tell me everything is going to be

203

ok Adrian." "It's going to be fine and you're going to spend the day with my sister and mother and you ladies are going to have an amazing time." Rebecca knocked at the door and came in grabbing Norey by the hand, "Come on sis we got the best day planned."

Today I just feel amazing I have everybody I love under one roof. I pushed dad in his wheelchair out to the van. Once I got him strapped in I ran back in to get his medicine. Norey pulled me to the side, "Please be careful, your family is great but to be honest, I just don't trust those rednecks from the meeting." "It's going to be fine, I'm going to have Vegas move our things into the guest house," I said as I rushed out the door. The members of the other families didn't want to meet at my father's farm because they knew that we were aware it was one of them who ordered the hit on me and my taste for revenge was far worst then my fathers. They didn't only try and murder me they turned my kind-hearted wife into a killer.

We arrived at the location of the meeting which was an odd place if you ask me. It was an old abandoned catholic church. I got dad out and pushed him inside. There were five luxury vehicles outside, two black escalades, a limousine, a navy-blue luxury van like dads and a fifteen-passenger van which was kind of odd for a simple meeting with my sick father. No worries though, I wheeled dad right passed the well-dressed Italians standing by the vehicle looking at me like they wished I would drop dead right there. "Dad, maybe we should have spaghetti tonight," I said. "I don't like that shit no more it tastes like ass," Dad said as the Italian men opened the door for us. I laughed and the man holding the door looked at us and spit on the ground. As I pushed dad towards the sanctuary of the church where the men who were clearly the leaders of the Mafia families sat surrounded by cigar smoke. They all looked back at us and started to whisper. I pushed dad to the very front at the altar and turned him towards the other Bosses and stood to the right of his chair. There were five old men there that my father introduced me to. "Adrian, this is Anthony Moretti of Brooklyn, New York. This one is Nicky Bianchi of Queens, New York. The old man with the funny look on his face is Paul Esposito of Long Island, New York. That one right there that's smoking a cigar in a house of worship is Don Ricci out the Bronx. Last but not least my oldest friend in the world Don Paul Puccini of Newark, Jersey.

"Lovely introduction Delruso but can your help wait outside I'd like to get down to business," said Paul Puccini. They all laughed, my Dad put his head down and exhaled then looked up in anger. "This is not the help, this is my son!" he shouted while coughing badly. I stood there firmly while making eye contact with each of the men. "I told you he lost his fucking mind," said Don Puccini as he glanced at Anthony Moretti. "I'm not begging you to love my son because that's my job. I will ask that you give my son a chance because all of us in this room needed a chance at least once in our life?" asked dad. He spent a lot of time trying to convince these people but I knew they didn't care if I could do the job or not, if I couldn't change the color of my skin they didn't want anything to do with me. I had told Norey that I wouldn't be long and it's been a few hours so I know she worried. My phone has been vibrating like crazy I know it's her and to be honest, I'm a bit worried too. I need to get dad home and I'm starting to wonder if these assholes have any intentions of letting us leave here.

Dad said answering phones or making phone calls are forbidden in these meetings. From the look on dad's face and the way he just grabbed my hand squeezed and then said I love you he thinks we're never leaving this church. I leaned down and whispered in Dad's ear than I stood up, "I know my skin color comes as a surprise to you.

If the opportunity is given I won't let you down. I'm not asking you to like the decision my father has made in appointing me to lead the Delruso family, but I am asking you to respect his dying wish. I'm coming to the table with an open mind and a fair heart and I'm hoping you will do the same." "Well put, let's go son."

The New York bosses looked at me as if I was some wild animal on their front lawn. As I pushed dad towards the exit I looked back and the old men were peeking their heads out the door looking from the room we just had the meeting in. They were watching us so hard their eyes were burning a hole through my blazer. My dad took his oxygen mask off as I pushed him towards the opening doors. "I'm sorry son, I'm so sorry. Maybe I should've left you and your family in New York," he said. "No dad, I'm glad you brought us home. They just fucked with the wrong family," I said as my father looked through the opening doors. I looked back at the old men and smiled as they slowly walked towards the doors in disbelief. Dad said I couldn't make or receive calls during the meeting but he didn't say I couldn't have HardRain tail us to find the location of the meeting. In the parking lot of the church, the five welldressed Italian guys were face down on the ground. The other fifteen in the bus van was trapped like caged rats. They were surrounded by Big Bail with 20 of the men from the Juke Joint and HardRain with 20 of his men from the Aryan brotherhood. Dad laughed and shook his head. He slowly struggled to stand up from his wheelchair turned and looked at the old men, "if it's fighting you're looking for, were Delruso's and we'll damn sure give you one," he said as he put his oxygen mask back on his face.

We got in the van and left, I finally got to check my phone. I had missed calls from Norey, mom, Rebecca and Vegas. It wasn't because they were worried; it was because Norey had gone into labor. "Dad, Noreen's having the freaking baby!" I shouted. "Why the hell you talking about it son, put the pedal to the medal, let me see my grandbaby!" We rushed to the hospital it was amazing.

Mrs. Sharon took tons of pictures. "My God he looks just like Adrian when he was a baby," said Mrs. Sharon. "Ain't

God good," said Rebecca. I rubbed Norey's hair and kissed her on the nose. Dad held the baby, "Thank you God for allowing me to see one of my grandchildren." This by far was the best night of my life.

Mom and Rebecca took dad home. I spent the night at the hospital with Norey and the baby. The next morning, we couldn't wait to get back home. I was so happy Norey had the baby when she did because dad passed away right after that. Mom was fixing his breakfast, and when she went to take it to him he was gone. We heard her screams all the way in the guest house. Between Dads passing away and the threatening letters in the mailbox about her grandbaby, she isn't really in a good emotional space right now. Those New York motherfuckers even went as far as taking a black doll baby cutting the head off of it, setting it on fire and leaving it on the hood of mom's van. Dad made me promise him before he died that I'd set it straight and I have their payback on its way right now.

Don Puccini's beloved grandson goes to a private school in Raleigh, North Carolina. I'm not an animal I don't believe in harming women and kids but I don't know if they're serious about hurting mine or not. Puccini's grandson has been missing about two days now and his daughter is losing it. I kind of figured he was going to send his best killers for me this time because he thinks I might have something to do with it. He can't go to the police because that'll be breaking the rules now won't it.

Dad's funeral is tomorrow, it's about 10:30 at night and I'm guessing me coming up dead on the day of Dad's funeral sounds like a pretty good statement for Puccini to make. Well someone should have informed him that we take our hunting pretty serious down here and we can sit in the woods for hours hunting one deer. We were out here since 9:00am watching the city boys drive back and forth past my driveway. It's just me, HardRain, Big Bail,

Whiteboy Vegas, and Loose Tooth Asshole. They call him Loose Tooth Asshole because his mother always yelling at him saying he will never get married because of his teeth being destroyed by meth. Loose tooth Asshole is the biggest asshole you ever seen but, the sumbitch can shoot a dime off a clothes line on a rainy day.

Now watch how he about to shoot the tire out on this Lincoln town car with New York plates that keep going back and forth down Delruso lane. Bong! The town car came to a slow stop. Four men got out in nice suits, one kicked the tire, "Damn it, Pauli, we drove down the same fucking street so much we got a fucking flat tire!" he said. "We're in the fucking middle of nowhere who the fuck is going to see us, don't worry!" said Pauli. "Nothing's dumber than a Yankee in the south," whispered HardRain. I laughed because it's kind of true. We were sitting here for hours in full camouflaged suits literally a few feet from them. We heard one of them say, "Put the window up these damn mosquitoes are killing me," as they passed by. "Let's just kill this nigger so we can get the fuck out of here," said Pauli. I looked over at HardRain, "Remind me to send Roy a care package over to the gas station. I'd probably be dead tonight if he didn't call and say there was Yankees down here filling up."

We waited until they got into my driveway and then we crept across the road into the blueberry field. They were looking around but couldn't see a thing because I had turned out all my porch lights. I also gave little Brandon twenty dollars to shoot out the streetlight with his pellet gun earlier that day. We laid flat on the ground with our shotguns pointed at the men while HardRain cut through the field and came around the other side of the house. "Come here guinea-guinea-guinea, come here guinea, guinea-guinea," he whispered. "What the fuck is that shit?" asked Pauli. "I don't fucking know!" his friend whispered aggressively. They started walking towards HardRain to see where the noise was coming from. That's when we ran out the field cocking back our shotguns and HardRain popped up off the lawn. "Where the fuck did you come from?" Pauli asked nervously. "Take'em to the barn," I said. HardRain grabbed Pauli by the face, "You don't know how happy it makes me, to catch me a Yankee, my daddy would be proud," he whispered.

I went inside the house and got dad's golf bag and walked out to the barn. When I walked in the four New Yorkers were chained by the wrist. Their arms were in the air, the chain was thrown across a weight bearing pole in the roof and hooked to Dad's old truck engine. The men were bleeding badly and they were scared. I mean I've seen men scared before but this was a different kind of scared. Men in our line of work usually are soldiers all the way to the grave but not these. Then I looked over at Loose tooth Asshole standing in the corner. He had a camouflage hat on with his shotgun across his shoulder. He was picking his nose with a huge smile showing all of his teeth that the meth just ate like they were candy. I just laughed hysterically about five minutes because I knew. These city boys were in a real nightmare and they didn't know shit about life down here.

I sat in pops favorite chair at the coffee table while HardRain was heating up the end of a dog chain with a blow torch. He looked over at Pauli, "Now I'm going to ask you one time, who sent you here and why? If you don't answer or you hesitate or I even believe you telling me a lie I'm gone strike you down the middle of your back with the wrath of God Almighty," he said passionately. Whiteboy Vegas looked over at me as if he thought I should stop it before it gets out of hand. It didn't take long for Pauli to start talking. "Puccini," he whispered as HardRain walked over with the burning orange hot chain. "Puccini, Puccini!" he shouted. "He told us to put down that ape, that a nigger would never run the Mafia," he said. "Don't you understand Mr. Delruso wasn't just any man in the mob, he was the most powerful man in the mob!" his friend shouted. I stood up and walked towards the man pulling my biological dad's ax from the golf bag I kept it in. "Who's responsible for the burned doll baby on my mother's car?" I asked. "Puccini, he ordered us to do it to warn you that they'll attack your family too if you don't step down," he shouted while crying uncontrollably. I began to scream hysterically and swung the ax several times with all my might. The men skulls popped like squished blueberries. We cut apart their bodies and put them in trash bags then drove them over to the funeral home where my dad's body was.

My dad knew the owner they had did business for years so he let us right in. I took out my burner phone and recorded video of the decapitated heads of each of Puccini's hit men. Then I threw them in the furnace and cremated them. That morning Norey, Mom, Rebecca and I got dressed for dad's funeral. It was the longest ride ever. After the preacher said his sermon we said our goodbyes. I took the can out of the paper bag I was carrying and placed the ashes of Puccini's men at dad's feet and took video of that as well.

When we got back into the limo to go home I sent the video to Don Puccini. Afterward, I called Loose tooth asshole's older brother Crunchy and told him to do it now. Crunchy had snatched Don Puccini's Grandson and drove him up to New Jersey in one of our blueberry trucks. Malcolm had just got out of prison and was hungry for some action so I had them build a casket and drill air holes in it. Crunchy and Malcolm tied up the kid and stuffed him in the casket with a 17 South road sign. They just dropped the casket off on Puccini's doorstep and rang the doorbell. Word around town was that some New Yorkers was trying to hire every hit man in the south it seems just to murder little ole me. That's cool, but what they don't know is down here it's not so much the drugs as it is the land. You see every crime family in the south survive through us. We own the fields, we own the trucks, and we own the distribution. Now guess what the last text message I sent to Don Puccini was…"Welcome to my zoo!!!"

Things have been quiet down here lately, and I know most people from the big city find comfort in that but not me. There's different types of silence down here and if you listen hard enough you can hear the chaos in it. The silence that I'm hearing now could mean a few things. One, somebody tied up in their own house because some junky need a hit and decided to break in. Two, somebody been dead for days and nobody found them yet. Three a mother fucking storm is coming! Word came from the bayou that the Puccini family has declared absolute war. Mr. Delruso had a friend named Gator John from New Orleans, he moved out west to open a shoe store. There's a high demand for Gator skin shoes out there so he decided to capitalize on it.

From what I hear Puccini is trying to make good on all his debts out west with hopes that his good deeds will bring more allies. If I remember correctly Malcolm is connected out in Cali, I did a few odd jobs for some friends of his out there. If New York pulls this off it could be a serious game changer which means more soldiers and more guns coming after my family. I knew the gloves would come off when I made that last move against The Puccini Family. Whatever sit-down is happening in California, it's a must I am there, and I would prefer to come to a peaceful resolution. Maybe by having a mediator from the west it could turn out to be a good thing. The war that's happening has everyone on edge and that's terrible for business I'm sure we all agree on that. People coming up missing got all of our families worried and with good reason because we haven't seen Loose Tooth Asshole in three days.

TWENTY-ONE

FOURTY DAYS OF DEMONS

Over the last year, sleep hasn't come easy. It seems like every sin I've ever committed is starting to haunt me in my dreams. I'm so irritated I decided to punch the bathroom mirror yesterday morning, cutting my hand and left with the images of my bloodshot eyes in the broken pieces. Knowing I'm suffering is bad enough, but when you add the fact I'm hiding being tormented by PTSD from Norey is horrible. How do I tell her that I keep seeing the faces of enemies I murdered? How do I tell her that I smell gun powder of those I shot and smell the blood of those I buried? Sometimes I hear the cries of their loved ones because I had the audacity to attend some of their funerals.

I feel like I'm stuck in a bad dream and nothing seems real anymore. I sweat so hard my pillow feels like it came out the washer. I'm constantly kicking and jumping in my sleep, waking Norey up on a regular basis. My snoring has become irritating; it keeps my wife and daughter ready to make me sleep in the barn. The worst part is the paranoia. In the world I live, where everyone is a potential danger, it has become hard to separate what's in my head and what's real. I went to the cemetery to visit mom, I really need her to talk to God for me. When I pulled back into the driveway today I saw Mrs. Sharon and Norey working in the flower bed on the side of the house. I smiled, took my seat belt off and took a deep breath; thank God, my family loves me because I have to come clean about what is happening to me.

I got out my black pickup truck and walked over to help them with the flower bed. "How are you feeling today son?"

Mrs. Sharon asked. "Well-," I whispered. "Are you ok babe?" Noreen asked. Everyone stopped what they were doing and stood up. I started to pull off my Carolina blue button up shirt while looking at the bag of dirt sitting in the wagon hooked to the lawn mower. "I'll just come out and say it, I haven't been feeling too well," I said. "Are you sick baby, because you look fine?" Noreen asked. "I've been restless, been having a lot of terrible dreams and really haven't slept well in months," I replied. "I see, you know Martin went through the same thing for a while and Azzy said your father went through it as well," Mrs. Sharon quickly responded. "Mom, did it go away?" I asked. "Yes it did, Azzy taught them about water fasting, have you heard of that?" "I've heard of it but I never knew much about it," I said. "I do, in my village back home the men would fast for 40 days after a war and after the hunting season. They say it helps to cleanse the spirit of death from your energy and allows God to enter a clean vessel," Noreen said.

That afternoon Norey and Mom went to the market and picked up some ammonia and a few cases of bottled water. They also stopped by the church and got some anointing oil from Reverend Moore. That night Mom put the anointing oil on my forehead and around the house. Norey took the battery out my phone and ran me a hot bath with a few capfuls of ammonia poured in it. Mrs. Sharon brought in a white cloth her and my real mom used to cover their heads with and pray when things were pretty bad. All the stuff they were doing was making me a little uncomfortable but it seemed like they were pretty confident, and it was making them feel better so I'm willing to try it. We got beside the bed and got on our knees, Mom and Norey shared her cloth, I took moms and Norey lead us in prayer. When we were done, to break the ice I started to joke about how no one wanted to get under my cloth with me because I had demons. We laughed and then I went to soak in my bath while Norey and Mom made them some coffee. As I bathed I heard a knock at the door, it was Vegas. Noreen told him I wasn't home, and honestly that made me feel bad because Norey and Mom knew how I was about my business. So for them to turn Vegas away meant they were feeling my pain and concerned. I soaked about an hour and really didn't feel any different. Norey and I laid in bed talking about how much she missed Africa lately. I love to hear her talk about her native country, I could listen for hours. My sister Rebecca crossed my mind because I haven't seen her in a few days. As a matter of fact, it seems I've been seeing her less and less the past few months.

As Norey was telling me about her visit to Cape Town, South Africa when she was seven years old I slowly dozed off. I had my head in Norey's arms peacefully asleep and suddenly my eyes opened wide and my body paralyzed in absolute fear. I had murdered Pauli a little over a year ago but here he is sitting on my dresser at the foot of my bed holding my daughter Cam'jor. There's blood oozing from the gash in his forehead that I put there with my father's ax. I'm pretty sure he's dead, I watched him die, and dismembered his body! Cam'jor screamed in fear as she reached for me, but I couldn't move. I tried to get up off the bed, almost straining my brain 'til it burst. My mama Azzy stood in the corner shaking her head in disappointment as she wiped the blood from the man I shot at the railroad tracks by my house when I was just a kid. I tried to say I was sorry but no words would come out, it was like I was on mute. I started breathing shallow for a few seconds then I began gasping for air as Mama Azzy, Pauli and the man from the tracks began to laugh at me. They began to slowly walk out the room shaking their heads while mama Azzy kept saying come on home son, come on home.

 I started to realize this can't be a dream because I can feel the tears running down my face. Cam'jor suddenly screamed out crying, so loud I jerked up from the bed with all of my strength. It was a dream, as I sat up on the bed covered in sweat Norey and mom was with some clean-cut white man in glasses standing by the bed crying. I had been sleeping for two days, and at first, they just thought I needed the rest, that was until I started kicking and screaming and they couldn't wake me up. Norey had called the ambulance but they couldn't find anything wrong. This kept happening for about a month, it took all my joy. I couldn't sleep, eat, or even breathe in my sleep sometimes. I gained weight and a lot of it because I would sit in my room eat and drink Jack Daniels so I wouldn't dream but the demons always came back. I haven't shaved or taken a bath in over a month. I only eat snacks that are in sealed bags and drink from sealed containers like soda or bottled water. The paranoia is to the point I think Norey and mom are trying to poison me so I don't eat their cooking. I overheard Big Bail in the kitchen this morning, so I stood by the bedroom door wrapped in my blanket eavesdropping. I could hear him asking about a trip we had planned to go to California for a meeting next week. He said everyone was getting concerned because no one has seen or heard from me in a month. He said some are wondering am I even still alive and as bad as I want to swing that fucking door open and shout I'm right here motherfucker and I'm never going to let them bastards' takeover, I can't. I just slid down the door and cried. Big Bail left and Norey came to the door trying to get in because she could hear my cry but I wouldn't let her in. "I love you, and I have to go to South Carolina for a few days but don't worry Rebecca is going with me while Mom stays here with you," she cried. I put a hand on the door knob and my hand started to tremble as tears ran down my face, I couldn't open it. "I love you!" I screamed to the top of my lungs as I fell to the floor wrapped in my blanket and curled up. All I know is Norey left, days have passed and I haven't moved from this spot. I pissed, shit and attempted to sleep in this same spot. My heart seems like it's slowing down and my dreams are starting to lose their color. It's been forty days and I'm pretty sure I'm dying today.

TWENTY-TWO

DEATH FROM THE BAYOU

It's Sunday morning, as I lay here in my own piss and shit all I can think about is I can clearly say its Sunday morning. I haven't been able to positively say what day it was for weeks now. As I inhaled the overwhelming stench in which I have laid in, I became sick to my stomach and began to vomit. I stood up, and even though I was disgusted with the conditions in which I've lived in the last several weeks, I was amazed at the strength and how refreshed I felt. I put on my robe, quickly grabbed a sheet from the closet and started picking up all the filthy linen and trash on the bedroom floor and tying it in a clean sheet. A feeling of shame came over me as I started thinking about Norey and Mom seeing me in this condition for all this time. They must think I had a nervous breakdown or that maybe I wasn't strong enough to continue with dad's legacy. They must think I'm weak, and my wife must be so embarrassed and feel like I let her down. I took the tied-up sheet and quietly tiptoed down the hallway hoping no one would hear. I walked out the back door and took the sheet and threw it on back my truck. I couldn't believe how good the sun felt on my face so I stopped, looked up and closed my eyes to enjoy the moment for a few seconds.

When I opened my eyes, there was Norey, mom and Rebecca staring out my bedroom window.

At first I felt a sudden embarrassment and held my head down but when I looked up Norey had put her palm on the window, the tears in her eyes with a smile of relief on her face let me know everything was going to be ok. I walked back into the house and went straight to the bathroom. There was a fresh towel, a bath cloth and a new set of clothes. As I reached for the sliding door on the shower there was a yellow piece of paper stuck on it that said, "I thought that I couldn't possibly love you and appreciate you anymore than I already did but you have shown me that my love for you is endless because today I love you even more than before," Love Norey. I smiled and honestly, I felt stronger, it was like I was reborn and never again would I not appreciate the life I have. I got into the shower and as the hot water hit my body I inhaled deeply and exhaled all of my troubles.

I started thinking about how grateful I was God gave me my health back and how I was going to live every day like I was grateful as well. First thing I need to do is apologize to my immediate family and then my extended family for my absence as well as my behavior. After my shower, I brushed my teeth and as I looked in the mirror I could see the light turned back on in my eyes. I think that's the part that scared me most when I was sick, when I looked into the mirror my eyes looked like I didn't have a soul anymore, it was like I wasn't even looking at me. I started getting dressed and smelled breakfast cooking and it seemed like forever since I could tolerate the smell of food. For the last few weeks the slightest smell of cooked food would make me throw up and become dizzy. I feel like I haven't eaten in years so I came out the bathroom and went straight to the kitchen. I could smell a heavy scent of Lysol as I walked down the hallway. Apparently while I was in the bathroom Mom, Rebecca and Norey decided to mop the floors, make the bed and of course from the anointing oil sitting on the kitchen counter, Mom has blessed the room as well.

"Hey Bro," Rebecca shouted as she hugged me. "I was so worried, I'm so glad you're feeling better," Mom said as she held me and didn't really want to let go. "I prayed so much," said Norey with tears in her eyes. "I'm ok, everything is going to be ok I promise," I replied as I kissed her. "So, we have all your favorites' blueberry pancakes, sausage, grits, biscuits and corn beef hash!" Mom yelled. We sat down and not a moment too soon because my mouth was watering from the smell of the food. We joined hands and as I said grace I could hear the exhaling happening around the table, they knew the storm had passed. We began to eat and as usual I made a joke out of the situation to break the uncomfortable vibe about discussing the situation. "Thought I was a goner didn't you sis?" I said with a laugh. "Yea, thought you was going beside the collard greens next to Nana," she replied as we all laughed. "Adrian, there's something we need to tell you," Norey said with a very serious look on her face. The bottom just fell out of my heart and fear froze every bone in my body as I stared at her knowing what we had just been through, what in the hell could put that look on her face.

"Big Bail came by while you were sick, he was a little worried about a trip you guys had planned for California. He also told me to tell you to be careful and even though we all know you don't believe in certain stuff to keep an eye on Gator John, your friend from New Orleans. He said his Mama Miss. Chaney told him to stay clear of you because she knows Gator John's Mother Miss. Doris, and she is heavy into Voodoo. He said someone offered Gator John $250,000 to kill you. He said Gator John knew he couldn't come at you directly so he convinced Miss. Doris to put a curse on you. To try and kill you in a way no one would notice. He said when you meet with Gator John about setting up the California trip he supposed to leave a rusty nail taped under your dashboard and to bring back something that belonged to you to Miss. Doris," Norey said with fear in her eyes.

I stood up from the table and shook my head. "What's wrong Adrian?" Rebecca asked. "I already had that meeting," I replied as I walked toward the front door. I went to my truck opened the driver's door, looked under my dash and there it was, a rusty nail duck taped under my dashboard right over my brake pedal. I paused for a second, confused because this just can't be real. I turned and looked at Norey, Mom and Rebecca in absolute shock. "If this shit is real or even possible that means I could be dying, how in the hell do I stop some shit like that?" I asked. Anger came over me as I rubbed my hands together listening to Norey. I quickly walked into the house grabbed a few clothes and began throwing them into my duffle bag. "I'll be back in a few days, I love you," I yelled to Norey as I darted out the house. I hopped into her tan Cadillac STS and went to pick up Big Bail, HardRain and Whiteboy Vegas. I couldn't believe that Gator John, my father's friend, would try to kill me and even worse what he had forced Norey and Rebecca to do.

Norey had been trying to connect with some people from her old village in Cameroon, Africa. She had found a few of the families who knew her as a child from the other villages. They gave her closure even though no one survived from her village. She did find the little girl she was rooming with at

234

the embassy when she and her grandmother escaped. They called her Sissy, her and Norey had become pen pals over the last year and swore they would visit. Norey wrote to her in Africa about what had happened and even though it wasn't what Norey wanted to hear she told her how to fix it. Norey told Rebecca about what Sissy had said in her letter so they agreed that even though it sounded insane they would drive down to South Carolina where Miss. Doris lives to try and convince her to take the hex off because it was killing me. Norey and Rebecca found Miss. Doris' information pretty easily, especially since everything is public knowledge these days on the internet.

They drove down to South Carolina, asked a few questions to the locals and sure enough our good ole southern hospitality pointed them right to her front door. Norey was hesitant when they pulled into the driveway because the whole voodoo story Big Bail had told her sound a little ridiculous to be honest but they had nothing else left but to give it a try. Rebecca quickly jumped from Moms navy blue caravan and walked right up and knocked on the door. Norey watched and shook her head as the door to the house opened slowly and an old gray-haired lady appeared at the door squinting to see Rebecca's face. They talked for a second and then Rebecca signaled to Norey to come on. As they slowly walked into the old house they clung tightly to one another's arm. Rebecca's face frowned up because of the strong smell of bengay and green rubbing alcohol mixed with the scent of pork neck bones cooking on the stove.

"So, what can I help you pretty young ladies with today? Don't be scared I don't bite just excuse the mess, I don't really get to much company these days," explained Miss. Doris. "I see why," said Rebecca while Norey nudged her on the hip to be quiet. As they stood tightly bundle by the couch looking around the room at all the creepy things in the house that Miss. Doris used in her so called black magic, they noticed a picture on a shelf of Gator John and his Mother. "See something interesting, go ahead take a look at it. What is it you need, is your boyfriend cheating, or is he beating on you honey, maybe somebody wronged ya, no matter what it is dollface I can fix it, ain't a limit to what I can do?" Miss. Doris whispered. Rebecca sat on the couch in front the old lady as Norey slowly started walking around the living room looking at all the creepy concoctions laying around.

"I have a friend, he's very sick. He locked himself in the room and won't come out. He's been using the bathroom on himself because he's too paranoid to be around people. He won't eat and he can't sleep because of his dreams, he keeps seeing people that he lost," Rebecca said. "How long has your friend been this way?" asked Miss. Doris as she chuckled a little. "About three months and it's getting worse," Rebecca replied. "Sounds like somebody got him fixed good honey, sound like he got one foot in the grave," Miss. Doris said. Norey stood behind the recliner that Miss. Doris sat on and she stopped in her tracks and looked directly

237

at Rebecca when she heard what was said. "You know my son, I can't help but notice you keep glancing over at his picture?" Miss. Doris questioned. "No, we're not from around here, so how would you help the person that was fixed or whatever?" asked Rebecca. "You can't honey, the only way to do that is to get the person who did it to take it off or if the person who did it dies, now where you say you gals come from again?" Miss. Doris asked. "Well-," said Rebecca. "Wait a minute, my youthful looks may just be gone but my mind still here," Miss. Doris said as she breathed heavily trying to hurry and stand up from her chair.

"Slow down old lady don't fall," Norey said. Miss. Doris stood and looked at Rebecca and then looked at Norey, "Get out of my house!" she shouted as she walked aggressively toward Rebecca. "Calm down lady," Rebecca shouted. "You Delruso's took everything my family had when you took our land and now I'm going to take everything you have, I'll never see death by the hands of a Delruso!" Miss. Doris shouted as she raised a hand full of a white powder-like substance to toss in Rebecca's face.

"Well how about you see death by the hands of Cameroon," Norey said as she wrapped her arm around Miss. Doris' throat and plunged a butcher knife from the counter deep into her back twisting it both ways. Rebecca and Norey knew they had been asking for directions around the small town they just murdered Miss. Doris in, and everybody in Paris Island, South Carolina sort of knew one another. They carried Miss. Doris' body into the woods behind her house and buried her. No one would notice she was missing for a while because she never had visitor's other than her son, and unfortunately for him I'm on my way to New Orleans to say hello to my father's old friend Gator John as we speak.

COMING SOON

Shade Tree Mafia "Bastards of Babylon"

With the biggest meeting of his life ahead of him, Adrian Delruso is on edge due to the betrayal of a longtime family friend. The New York Mafia wants him dead now more than ever and will do anything to stop him. The Los Angeles meeting is vital and will determine who has unlimited access to Mexico's most powerful Cartels. Whoever makes this alliance will become unstoppable and their enemy will become dead. Adrian Delruso and his wife Noreen Delruso will travel to Africa to meet the only person left alive that knew Noreen's family who was murdered when she was a child. Finally, able to relax and enjoy the quiet and the beauty of Noreen's native country, a storm like no other is about to rip through the Delruso Family when one of their own will come face to face with a violent death.

AFTERWORD

This novel is a work of fiction and in no way, do we condone violence and hatred in our communities. Too many have lost their lives and too many families have lost loved ones. This novel is for entertainment and hopefully you can walk away with some information that will help you see life through a different lens. The bond built between some of the characters are unbreakable even though their obstacles are almost unbearable. I love how, the love that the family shares are more important than the blood they share.

The friendship between Azzy and Mrs. Sharon is tested when the communities they live in turns on them and begin to attack them and their loved ones.

I love how the bond of siblings "Rebecca and Adrian" is almost color blind. I say almost because the only time color becomes a problem is when someone else makes it one. It's like that with Whiteboy Vegas as well; his loyalty to his childhood friend seems to not only be color blind but leaves him with no sense of danger. It's like he never had a second thought about helping his childhood friend stay alive.

I think one of my favorite parts is the bond between Adrian and his biological father. In almost every book or film today there's a negative light on the father. Either he is absent or in prison so the decision to have him as a strong figure in Adrian's life was important. Also, the back and forth between the words biological father and adopted father was intentional to show that Adrian had love and respect for both the male figures in his life. It was to show a small representation of today's blended family and how it's easier to let the child enjoy being loved and cared for by more than one person.

With that being said it brings me to the strong love that Adrian and Noreen shares. The struggles they faced were more than a lot of people could handle, but the truth is couples face these challenges in poverty every day. The beauty in the way that they're so concerned about one another's well-being and the way they're willing to put the other feelings and safety before their own. The way they are tested on a day to day basis and how you can go through the changes with them as they grow into adults is amazing. The way Noreen describes Cameroon makes you want to go there today.

I would have to say the way Adrian Delruso and HardRain are forced to build a bridge between their families in order for them all to survive is epic. By taking the last two people on earth who would ever see eye to eye and making the survival of their families depend on them building a friendship will leave you questioning every good deed. Most people would think this novel is about Gangsters, drugs and money but it's not. It's about what would you do if your whole world fell apart and when you look around the room the people you love most are looking at you, and counting on you! One of my favorite sayings is "A dog will eat his

own shit when he's hungry".

About the Author

Kenneth Thomas is a lover of the arts, music, film and writing. He has a passion for community activism and outreach. Kenneth serves as President of the B.O.L.F.F.A Foundation "Beacon of Light for Fallen Angels" and Host of the "Bolffa Radio Podcast."

STAY CONNECTED

Visit our website @ www.shadetreemafia.com

Connect with us on social media! #STMnovel

FACEBOOK: @STMnovel & @DelrusoFamily
(Feel free to tag us in your fb post of your photos with
your STM book.)

TWITTER: @shadetreemafia (Tweet us using
#STMnovel with a photo of you holding your book.)

INQUIRIES

Mickey Bentson

mickey@payupmanagement.com

www.payupmanagement.com

CPSIA information can be obtained
at www.ICGtesting.com
Printed in the USA
LVOW04s0637290917

550526LV00010B/182/P